"Excuse me, Mr. Johansen. Might we talk privately? I'd like to propose something to you."

As soon as the words popped out of her mouth, Rose regretted them. They'd come out all wrong—and with an audience, too. When would she ever learn to think first and speak second? She should have formulated her approach—that would have minimized the chances of his refusal.

This wasn't Chicago, she reminded herself, where she was known—and where her outspoken style was almost legendary. There, it didn't matter how blunt her words were. She was expected to speak her mind.

Here, though, she needed to be more prudent in what she said.

JANET SPAETH has loved to read for as long as she can remember, and romances were always a favorite. Today she is delighted to be able to write romances based upon the greatest Love Story of all, that of our Lord for us. When she isn't writing, Janet spends her time reading a romance or a cozy mystery, baking chocolate chip cookies, or spending precious hours with her family.

Books by Janet Spaeth

HEARTSONG PRESENTS
HP522—Angel's Roost
HP458—Candy Cane Calaboose

Rose Kelly

Janet Spaeth

Heartsong Presents

For my sister Pat, who understands me and still loves me!

A note from the Author:
I love to hear from my readers! You may correspond with me by writing:

Janet Spaeth
Author Relations
PO Box 721
Uhrichsville, OH 44683

ISBN 1-59310-848-6

ROSE KELLY

All scripture quotations are taken from the King James Version of the Bible.

All of the characters and events in this book are fictitious. Any resemblance to actual persons, living or dead, or to actual events is purely coincidental.

Our mission is to publish and distribute inspirational products offering exceptional value and biblical encouragement to the masses.

PRINTED IN THE U.S.A.

one

Jubilee, Dakota Territory—1879

Jubilee!

Only an inbred sense of decorum kept Rose Kelly from pressing her nose against the window of the train like an excited child.

She had been on this train much too long. Every shudder and shimmy made her tense, knowing that the dreadful grating of metal on metal was about to begin. She'd have no teeth left if the train didn't come to a complete stop soon. Her jaw ground right along with the shriek of the brakes and the wheels on the tracks.

The train grated to a squealing halt, and Rose tried to restrain herself from elbowing her way to the front of the passengers disembarking.

Jubilee!

Despite her exhaustion—who could sleep on a train that joggled and jiggled and screeched the way this one did?—she was anxious to see this place that would be her home for the next six months.

She'd been watching through the train window as Jubilee came into view. It was a tiny whistle-stop town in the Dakota Territory, a cluster of buildings huddled protectively together on the open prairie. In winter, such proximity might be a blessing. But now with the glorious summer sun pouring over the grassy expanse, such closeness seemed an excess.

The crowd surged forward, and she felt herself being propelled toward the exit. She grasped her signature bag, a tiny thing embroidered and beaded with pink and red roses, and let the movement carry her.

Suddenly she was squeezed out into the front, to the open door. . .and she stepped into air. The footing she thought would be there wasn't, and she dropped suddenly toward the platform.

The crowd pushed again, and in a most ungainly and unfeminine move, she was launched into a very solid shape. Two arms came out of nowhere, it seemed, and caught her just before she hit the platform's surface. Strong arms. Tanned arms. Muscular arms.

"Careful, miss."

She looked up into blue eyes that exactly matched the Dakota sky behind him. The wind ruffled his hair, as blond as summer wheat.

He quickly dropped his arms. . .and his gaze.

"Wanted to make sure you weren't injured," he muttered. "Are you going to be all right?" he asked, and she realized that she was still clutching his arms.

Rose considered her rescuer as she released her grip and adjusted the front of her traveling suit—quite the thing back in Chicago. This man might be a good resource for her needs.

"Is someone coming for you?" he asked, but his words were more a statement than a question, as if he already knew the answer. His forehead knotted into a frown. From the lines etched there, Rose thought that expression must be a perpetual state with him.

"No." She looked at her surroundings. Even with all the research she'd done before coming out, nothing had prepared her for this.

What she'd seen from the train had been deceptive. Jubilee was more than a nervous clump of buildings. It was a genuine town with genuine buildings and genuine people walking on genuine streets.

Oh, there was a rough, raw edge to it, but Jubilee was definitely a town that would still be on the map in a century or two.

"Miss?"

With a start, she realized that she remained standing in front of the train exit and was being buffeted by the other passengers trying to leave the train.

"Are they all coming here?" she asked as a passenger's oversized carrier bashed her leg. She'd have a large bruise there by nightfall.

Taking her arm, he adeptly moved her out of the human traffic. "Just for a moment." A trace of a smile lit those sky-blue eyes. "I suspect they're anxious to feel solid land under their feet."

"I know how they feel." Even though she was standing on a very flat, very stationary platform, her body still vibrated from the long ride. "This is the first real stop we've made today. The fresh air is wonderful. It gets a bit close inside the car after a while. I do believe I'd have gotten off even if this weren't my destination."

"You're visiting here?" Again, an inquiry that wasn't one.

"No." She pulled herself up to her full height. It wasn't much, just a bit over five feet. "I'm here on business."

A shadow of a frown wrinkled his brow. "Business? Here in Jubilee?"

His thoughts couldn't have been more obvious if his forehead were transparent. She could see him trying to figure out what kind of business would bring her to a town like

Jubilee. Etiquette struggled with curiosity, and etiquette won. He did not ask. She did not tell.

"Do you have lodging?" he inquired. "The best hotel in this area is the Territorial."

It's also the only hotel, she thought but didn't say. She had reservations at the Territorial, choosing what she hoped was some degree of privacy that she might not get in a boardinghouse.

"Would you like some help with your bags?" he asked.

Her reporter's eye had already taken in not just the obvious physical attributes of the man but the subtleties, as well. He didn't seem to be dangerous or aggressive. Her instincts weren't perfect, but they were generally good. Yet a certain wariness was, of course, in order.

"I can hire a wagon. I'll need to do that anyway." She glanced around. "If you can tell me where I might find one?"

"Clanahan's down the street is really the only place where you might find something like that. He has a few that he picked up from folks abandoning their claims and going back east again."

She visually measured the distance against the weight of her bags, then surveyed her surroundings as she realized she couldn't possibly carry her belongings that far. The area looked safe enough, although one could never be sure.

He must have seen her indecision, because he said with a touch of amusement in his voice, "You do know that the Territorial is across the road, don't you?" He pointed to a brick building behind the station.

How could she have missed it? It was the tallest structure in town.

She easily found her two bags. They were the only pieces of real luggage left in the pile of cartons and wrapped bundles on the platform. He reached for both of them, but she was faster and grasped the smaller of the bags herself. "I can carry this myself."

He didn't answer, but she was sure she saw a flicker of admiration on his face.

The hotel was far beyond what she had imagined she'd find in Jubilee. Three stories tall, constructed of brick so new that it was still hard-edged and clean, it was a sentinel on the prairie.

"This is it," he said unnecessarily as they paused beneath the large sign: TERRITORIAL HOTEL. ROOMS.

She dropped her bag and secretly flexed her fingers. The handle had pressed into her palm so completely that her fingers were numb. Had the hotel been much farther, she might have had to swallow her pride and let him help her carry the bag.

"Thanks for your help." She stretched her hand—the one that still had feeling in it—toward him.

"You're welcome."

He turned and began to walk away. But he returned. "You might need some more help with these bags." He easily hefted them up and carried them into the lobby toward the desk, where he deposited them. "Matthew can take care of them from here," he said, motioning to the young man behind the desk. "By the way," he added, "I'm Eric Johansen."

"Rose Kelly. It's been nice to meet you, and thanks again for your help with my bags." She smiled at him as a terribly rogue thought drifted into her head: *Too bad you're only staying here six months, Rose Kelly. He's got awfully nice eyes.*

&

Eric watched her through the window as she dealt with the Territorial's desk clerk. Matthew would take good care of her. He was a fair and decent man—Eric had seen that side of him often in church.

He had known from the moment she stepped off the train—and into his arms—that she was traveling alone. Her gaze hadn't swept the crowd at the station; instead, she'd raised her eyes to the buildings and beyond. That single movement had been quite telling.

From the corner of his eye, he saw Mrs. Jenkins and Mrs. Simmons, their heads together and their eyes staring directly at him. They hid their mouths behind their hands, but he knew what they were doing—undoubtedly talking about him and pairing him up with the guest.

He realized he probably shouldn't have carried her bags into the hotel, but what choice did he have? He couldn't leave her standing on the street.

With a quick sweep of his hat, he acknowledged the two women. Perhaps a direct response was best to forestall the rumors that were certainly already making their way through town.

They could talk all they wanted to. He had no time for a woman in his life, not now and, really, not ever.

He turned back to the station across the street, aware of the fact that he'd totally forgotten to pick up the plow part that had come on the train.

No, he had no time for women. Not even for someone with eyes that sparkled with green and golden flecks and with hair that caught the summer sunlight like new copper.

He shook his head. Next thing he knew, he'd be abandoning farming for poetry.

It was time to bring his head back to earth. Fast.

☙

Rose surveyed her room. It was more than she'd expected.

Actually, it was quite lovely in a basic sort of way. Although it admittedly couldn't hold a candle to the suites of her favorite Chicago hotel, the extremely elegant Palmer House, it certainly outshone the grimy rooms she'd seen in New York and Boston. The absolute newness of it was quite charming.

She sank to the bed and took stock of her situation. It was amazing that she was even here.

She'd never had even the vaguest intention of coming out to the Dakota Territory to begin with. If only she hadn't overheard her editor, George Marshall, at the *Chicago Tattler* telling one of his male reporters that no woman could do what he had in mind.

Those had been fighting words, and she'd barreled right in, arguing with Mr. Marshall, the whole time having no idea what she was shouting about.

Her daddy had always said that Rose was born with the Kelly temperament—yell first, ask questions later—and while her mother sighed helplessly into her apron and turned back to an endless array of diapers and socks when Rose announced her plans, she'd caught a glimpse of a smile on her father's face. He was proud of her.

It was her natural inquisitiveness, he'd told his friends, that made her a crackerjack reporter, and he had puffed out his barrel chest proudly when he told them of her accomplishment. His daughter, he proclaimed, was heading off to the land of wonder and adventure—the Dakota Territory.

Her mother hadn't been so convinced. Although Katie Kelly was not one to speak up, especially against her husband, her face spoke volumes. One eyebrow could shoot, quite independently of the other, to her hairline to indicate displeasure. Her eyes, once a warm kitten gray, were now faded and dim beneath lines etched deeply over the bridge of her nose.

But Rose saw something in her mother's eyes that escaped the gaze of her rambunctious brothers—the way the eyebrows settled and the gray softened when a baby was placed in her arms. Rose had seen the work-worn hands smooth a delicate blanket, noted the pain as a callused finger caught a fragile thread. And the sadness with which the baby was returned to the mother.

Katie Kelly had wanted babies, grandbabies, but Rose had wanted more.

She wanted to live in a whirlwind of excitement, always moving, always on the go, always finding out about things.

When Mr. Marshall had almost laughingly offered Rose the job of covering the fashion gossip scene, she'd seized it eagerly. Almost every week she attended a party, and eventually the elite of the city took her presence at their functions as a societal coup.

Everybody wanted Rose Kelly at their gatherings.

She had done well, had earned the right to be a reporter, and she knew she was a pioneer in her field. She got letters every week from girls who wanted to be her when they grew up.

Now she wanted to do more.

The heated discussion she'd had with a bemused Mr. Marshall resulted in just that. She'd had to plead her case, even when she found out that at stake was a series of articles about homesteading in the Dakotas.

Truth be told, she hadn't wanted it, but when it sounded like Mr. Marshall was going to give the assignment to Jerrold Pugh, a whiner if she'd ever heard one—and a self-important whiner, to boot—she'd had to leap right in and wrench the assignment away from him.

And now she was here, ready to get to work. A shiver of excitement shot down her spine as she considered how to proceed.

Could it be that God had given her the subject of her articles? Might it be Eric Johansen?

It was a splendid idea.

She stood up and went to the lace-trimmed window. Her room faced away from the center of Jubilee, and from her window, she saw an amazing green vista.

The summertime prairie looked like it had awakened from a long nap, stretched out its deep brown lengths, and sprouted.

She chewed her lip as she thought about Eric.

Rose wasn't ignorant of men. Not at all. Working at the *Chicago Tattler*, she was surrounded by men. Admittedly, most of them were cigar-smoking, middle-aged men whose primary concerns were how Chicago's baseball team, the White Stockings, were doing and whether the beer would be cold at Albert's, the neighborhood tavern.

None of them seemed to consider her as anything other than one of the fellows. The thought gave her pause, but she shook it off. It was better that than they notice her female attributes. At least this way she was considered an equal.

In most things. Now, this assignment. . .

Eric didn't seem to view her the way the fellows she worked with did. There was something different, something she couldn't quite put her finger on.

Unexpectedly she yawned. She was really quite tired.

During the entire trip, she hadn't been able to sleep deeply. All she could do was close her eyes and drift off a bit.

Everything she saw from the train window was new and fascinating, and missing even a bit of it was out of the question. The journey was entirely too exciting.

Not that she intended to stay here. Once she was done being a paid tourist, she could go back to her rather comfortable home in Chicago and the excitement of a city that lived twenty-four hours a day. Meanwhile, she'd enjoy the peaceful calm of the prairie, where nothing moved except the grass in the wind.

She dropped onto the pristine pale blue coverlet and closed her eyes, just to think about her travels and her future and a man who seemed to be Dakota himself. . . .

two

My first impression of the Dakota Territory was that it is entirely blue and green. As I got off the train, I saw nothing but endless land that touched an equally endless sky. The world here is hemmed in only by our limited imaginations.

Which came first—the growling in her stomach or the aroma of something wonderful wending its tempting way under her door—didn't matter. Rose woke up with a roaring hunger gnawing at her stomach.

What a dream she'd had! A train ride that seemed never to end, a land that sprawled under a sunlit sky, eyes that caught that blue sky. . .

She rubbed her eyes and took in her surroundings. The plain but clean hotel room. Her bags, still unpacked at the door. The absence of street sounds from her slightly opened window. Sudden realization washed over her.

It wasn't a dream. No, not at all.

Jubilee!

Rose sprang out of bed and pressed her nose to the window. Yes, the glorious sunshine still poured across the prairie, and she fairly itched to get out there and take a look.

But first she had to attend to the scraping emptiness of her stomach. Some things didn't change, she thought as she checked her dress and made sure it wasn't too wrinkled to wear downstairs for dinner. One common trait of all the Kellys was what her father called "a healthy respect for the dinner plate."

15

Food first, exploration later.

She splashed water on her face and repinned her hair into its usual strict bun, which had gotten a bit scraggly during her nap. The only advantage of having the straightest hair in Chicago had been that keeping it styled was fairly easy. Her hair was never tempted to curl, so she'd made the knot of copper at the nape of her neck into her trademark hairstyle. Even for parties, she wore the same style and added a velvet bow as decoration.

She hadn't packed many velvet ribbons for her visit to Jubilee.

With a resolute poke of the final pin into her hair, she stood up straight, put her hands on her hips, and stared at her reflection in the gilt-edged mirror.

Her father's words came back to her. They'd been standing at the station, waiting for the train that would take her away for six months, when he pulled her close and boomed, "Well, Rose Kelly, you've done it now. You've put yourself in the midst of it, right into the wildest of the wild. The Dakota Territory. You won't be finding the parties and elegant dresses you're used to, not there." Then he grinned. "And I think, my darlin', that you're going to be the better for it. I'm proud of you."

Her mother had simply hugged her, tears pooling in her pale gray eyes. "God be with you."

Six months. She could do it. She would do it.

The enticing fragrance of baked ham drew her to the dining room of the Territorial. It was small, with the tables placed close together. The tables were topped with clean, starched white cloths that looked like thick cotton, and the sole decoration on each was a simple glass set of salt and pepper shakers.

Just last week she'd had lunch with a social belle at one of Chicago's newest restaurants, a tiny place along the lakeshore with an unpronounceable French name, where she'd dined on pheasant sautéed in some lovely sauce.

The baked ham here, though, smelled just as delicious.

A table by the window was empty, and as she made her way toward it, conversation in the room ceased, and in unison all heads swiveled toward her. A more reticent person might have ignored the obvious reaction she was causing, but Rose Kelly had never been reticent.

She smiled at all of them. "Hello, everyone," she caroled. "Is the food good? It smells wonderful!"

The other diners relaxed and smiled in response and once again began to talk at their tables. She proceeded to her seat, satisfied. This, she'd always believed, was the way to live. Being straightforward almost always worked best.

Bits and pieces of their discussions floated toward her.

"Arrived today. . ."

"Chicago. . ."

"Eric Johansen. . ."

She tried not to be too obvious as she shamelessly eavesdropped. Her eyes lit with a puckish glow as she realized that her fellow diners were, indeed, already linking her with Eric. It was too charming.

Matchmaking, were they?

Interesting. . .

❧

One last swing of the hammer, and the floorboard would be fixed. If only those Nielsen children would quit their constant wiggling during the service, the wooden slats might hold up better. They were the squirmiest young ones he'd ever seen.

But children would be children, he reminded himself, and

no matter how rambunctious they might be, they were a blessing from the Lord. The Nielsens came to church every single week to hear the Word and offer praise, Michael and Grethe leading their seven children in a stair-stepped line. He could only imagine what it must be like to get seven children dressed for church.

He dropped his head and offered a quick prayer for the family: *Dearest Father, please bless the Nielsen family for their constant faithfulness to You.* He peeped at the mended board and added, *And help me not to be so judgmental about fidgety children. Amen.*

Voices from the kitchen at the back of the church broke his reverie. He knew that a group of women were there, scurrying around in preparation for Sunday's after-church dinner.

He sniffed the air appreciatively as a tantalizing aroma drifted his way. If his senses weren't deceiving him, the women were making *lefse*, the delicious Norwegian treat. Maybe they'd have some to spare—for a man who was giving up his Saturday evening to mend a floorboard. He stood, unfolding slowly as his muscles, cramped from bending over so long, relaxed.

"Hello!" he called as he limped back to the kitchen, the feeling in his legs slowly returning. He was getting too old to be sitting on the wooden floor of the church, bent like a broken spring. "Do I smell lefse?"

Mrs. Jenkins poked her head out of the doorway, her snowy hair a bit disarranged and a smudge of flour across her cheek. "Eric Johansen, you're just in time. We're trying out a new *takke* that Grethe just got from her family back in Bergen, and we've finished the first batch. We need your opinion."

He had to smile. Just two years ago, nothing she said would have made any sense, but now that he was totally immersed in this heavily Norwegian community, it was absolutely clear.

"What's a takke?" a woman asked behind him. "And where's Bergen?"

"Miss Kelly," he said, recognizing her voice immediately. The impish smile on Mrs. Jenkins's face told him that the gossip mill had already started turning, and he groaned silently. This was the last thing he needed now, just when the land was taking up almost every moment of his waking hours—except those used mending cracked floorboards in the church: a woman in his life.

He turned and pasted on what he hoped was a pleasant yet noncommittal smile, but the woman before him nearly took his breath away.

Early evening sunlight, thick and rich as it came through the single stained-glass window in the church, poured across Rose's shoulders and head, casting ruby and emerald and sapphire shadows on her russet hair. She looked as if she had stepped right out of heaven.

Whoa, Johansen. Bring it under control. He dug one fingertip into his thumb to remind him that this was no dream, and she was no vision, and as a matter of fact, they were standing outside the kitchen of Redeemer Church in Jubilee with an overly interested audience. "It's very nice to see you again. I trust you're finding your lodging to your liking."

"The Territorial is an ideal hotel for my purposes," Rose answered, and she tilted her head slightly, questioningly, for a moment. Finally he realized that she was waiting for him to step aside so she could go into the kitchen. When he did, she touched his arm lightly with a tiny hand.

He didn't dare move. That hand on his arm was unexpected,

and he had no idea what to do. Leave it there? Brush it off? Step back?

It's not a spider, Johansen, he scolded himself. *What's the matter with you? She's just a woman.*

Just a woman. Well, that was the problem right there.

"Thank you for your help. I truly do appreciate it," she said, apparently unaware of the effect she was having on him, and she dropped her hand.

Before he could answer, she swept past him toward Mrs. Jenkins. "Hello," she greeted the older woman, who grinned back at her with delight. "My name is Rose Kelly, and I'm visiting from Chicago. . . ."

Almost as if an invisible force pulled him, he trailed after her.

"Series of articles. . .homesteading. . .newspaper."

He didn't catch all of the sentences, but he heard enough to piece together what her purpose was in Jubilee. So she was a newspaper reporter. That made sense—he guessed.

She certainly didn't seem the kind to be happy on the frontier, though, carving out a life in a prairie-dust town like Jubilee. There was something about her that bespoke money and class and comfort.

Maybe it was that ridiculous little bag she carried. He had no idea what it contained, but it was too tiny to hold anything of value, like the tine from a harrow or a bag of oats or even a cheese sandwich.

Maybe it held her money, but he hoped not. Certainly she would have taken care of that aspect with Matthew at the hotel and put her funds securely in the Territorial's safe.

"I'll be here for six months," Rose was saying.

Six months? He found himself counting—and then shaking his head. She was planning to leave when winter had settled in? Whose idea was that?

"So tell me what a takke is." Rose looked around the kitchen, and he was sure that even the tiniest detail didn't escape her examination. "I've never heard of one before. Where's Bergen, by the way?"

Mrs. Jenkins looped her arm through Rose's and walked her across the tiny kitchen. "Bergen is a town in Norway. That's where Grethe Nielsen is from. A takke is a pan we use to make lefse, and she's letting us use hers. She'd be here now except she has seven children, so she has her hands full as it is. But she's the champion lefse maker of Jubilee."

"Lefse. That's a new one for me. How do you spell it?" To Eric's amazement, she opened the rose-embellished miniature bag and pulled out not only a pen but a notebook as well. "And what is it?"

Mrs. Jenkins's words were a background of sound as he leaned against the doorway to the warm kitchen and watched Rose learn her first lesson in Dakota living. "Lefse is a Norwegian pastry," the older woman began. "It's made of potatoes and flour and butter and cream and—"

"Potatoes?" Rose interrupted. "Potatoes? You make a pastry out of potatoes?"

She leaned over and studied the pile of potatoes at the end of the metal table as if they held the secret to eternal youth. With the blunt end of her pen, she gave one an experimental poke and made a note on her pad.

Eric suppressed a grin. *City girl*, he thought.

"Oh yes, and potatoes make a lovely thick mix." Mrs. Jenkins loosened her grip on Rose long enough to point to a pile of dough. "There's some already made up. We take a bit of the dough like this and shape it into a ball. Then we roll it out evenly, as thin as possible, and carefully pick it up and put it on the takke. That's the hot grill there. Yes, we use that stick to pick up the dough and to turn it on the grill so it doesn't tear. See how it slides under the dough and lifts it just so... And when it's done, we call in Eric to test it."

Rose turned toward Eric and smiled widely.

He stepped into the room and reached for the lefse that was still suspended on the stick. "Yum," he said as he tore off a piece of it. "Lefse is good anytime, but when it's still warm, then it's the best. Try it."

He offered her the rest of the flat bread and watched as she popped it into her mouth. Would she like it?

"We sometimes put butter and sugar on it," Mrs. Jenkins said.

"I don't know why," Rose said, finishing it. "It's so good. Interesting, though. It doesn't taste at all like potatoes."

Mrs. Jenkins smiled. "No, it doesn't."

"May I ask another question? Why are you making so much of it?" Rose pointed to the piles of already-prepared lefse on the counter.

Mrs. Jenkins expertly lifted and turned another piece on the grill. "We're having a dinner here tomorrow. You're welcome to come."

"May I? It sounds like fun!" One of the last rays of sunlight slanted through the door, illuminating Rose's smile even more.

Mrs. Jenkins beamed. "You'll enjoy it. You'll find plenty of good food. Most of the folks in Jubilee have Norwegian roots, and that's why we make so much lefse. We don't do much *lutefisk,* though."

The other women in the small kitchen laughed.

"Lutefisk?"

Eric shook his head in amusement. "They're teasing you.

Lutefisk is a Norwegian dish, and while some people say it's wonderful, others refuse to eat it. Or to even be in the same room with it."

"Why?"

The women laughed louder.

"Well," he said, "it's rather. . .fragrant."

"But what is it?" Rose asked, her pen poised over her notepad.

"Mrs. Jenkins? Do you want to explain?"

The older woman said, "It's fish, usually cod, that's been dried and then soaked in lye."

The expression on Rose's face was wonderful. She looked from person to person, studying their faces. "You're joking with me, aren't you? There isn't any such thing as this lutefisk."

"I'm sorry, Miss Kelly," he said. "It's true. But most of us prefer lefse. There aren't any surprise ingredients in it, and it smells much better."

"Lutefisk? Sounds like it'd kill you," she muttered as she put her pen back in her bag.

"You might wish that, if you had to be around it," he said, and Mrs. Jenkins swatted him with a towel.

"Get out of my kitchen," she said, her words laced with laughter. "But first make sure that Miss Kelly knows that she's to come to the dinner tomorrow. I'm afraid she's fearful that there might be lutefisk."

"That'd be something to fear, all right." He turned to Rose. "There won't be any lutefisk tomorrow. You can expect chicken and ham and beef, but no lutefisk. Trust me. That stuff has a powerful stink."

"Eric, be nice." Mrs. Jenkins shook her finger at him. "Make Miss Kelly feel at home here. You're the first person she met in Jubilee, you know, and it should count for something."

Laughter bubbled through the woman's words, gentling the scolding with fond teasing.

Rose tilted her head and smiled at him.

He could feel his resistance crumbling, and he knew he should simply say something vague that no one could read anything into, bid them all good-bye, and turn around and walk away. That would be the best idea.

Instead, his mouth opened, all by itself, and began to speak. "The dinner is being held here on the lawn after church tomorrow." He could feel the women's gazes locked on him, and without looking at them, he knew that they were all smiling as they watched the tableau unfold before them. The words continued to pour out of his lips. "If you'd like to join us, we'd sure be glad to have you."

No! No! He didn't want to do this. What was he thinking? He knew the answer immediately: He hadn't been thinking.

Quickly he tried to recover his dignity—a task that was probably pointless, he thought, seeing the look on Mrs. Jenkins's face. "You may not go to church. I don't know. Especially out here in the Dakota Territory. We don't have the same grand churches you're probably used to in Chicago."

His words sounded ungracious, but Rose tucked her notebook back into that absurd little pouch and said, "Miss church? You must be joking. Patrick and Kathleen Kelly would have my own little head on a plate if I skipped a service. My parents raised me as a Christian, and I'm glad of it."

She looked directly at him, her eyes as green as a mossy rock, and added, "Everything I have, I owe to the Lord. Of course I'll go to church here. He doesn't forget me. Why should I forget Him?"

three

Every community has its own spirit, its own identity. The kind of place we call home tells us more about who we are than about where we are. Likewise, this visitor finds definition of who she is by determining who she is not.

Rose leaned across the stove and studied Eric. Even this early in the season, his skin was tanned to a dark honey by the sun, and his fingers were work-hardened with cuts and scrapes. His trousers and faded brown work shirt confirmed the image of him as a farmer.

But underneath the earth-stained man of the prairie, she sensed something else. A very solid thread she couldn't identify bespoke of a life beyond the prairie.

He'd be perfect for the assignment.

"Excuse me, Mr. Johansen. Might we talk privately? I'd like to propose something to you."

As soon as the words popped out of her mouth, Rose regretted them. They'd come out all wrong—and with an audience, too. When would she ever learn to think first and speak second? She should have formulated her approach—that would have minimized the chances of his refusal.

This wasn't Chicago, she reminded herself, where she was known—and where her outspoken style was almost legendary. There, it didn't matter how blunt her words were. She was expected to speak her mind.

Here, though, she needed to be more prudent in what she said.

Mrs. Jenkins and the other women in the room exchanged a silent but expressive round of glances. Silent laughter shook their plump chests, and from the discreet elbow nudges and the peeks at Eric and then her, she knew what they meant. They were pairing her off romantically with Eric.

She lowered her eyelids and studied him surreptitiously. *You could do worse,* came the unbidden thought. *As a matter of fact, you'd be hard pressed to do better.*

Wrong! Wrong! She was here to work, not to find a man. Chicago was full of men. If she wanted to go shopping for love, she should do it there. But there was something about this man, something interesting. *Something,* she chided herself, *that makes him a good subject for my articles.*

She realized she was staring at him. His cheeks were flushed, and he seemed to be uncomfortable with the attention.

The women quickly averted their gazes and turned their attention to the smoking griddle.

His clear blue eyes were clouded with a hint of wariness. "I'm probably going to regret this," he said in a low voice, nodding slightly to the women huddled over the takke, "but let's step outside."

He led her out of the small church into the summer evening. "I'd lay my life down for those women," he explained as they walked toward the hotel, "but they've been scrutinizing every woman who's set foot in Jubilee. Apparently they think I can't get my own woman."

"Can you?" Aghast at what she'd just said, Rose clapped her hand over her mouth. "Oh, I am so sorry! I didn't mean . . . Of course you can . . ."

To her amazement, he grinned. "That's all quite encouraging, but the issue is really that I'm not in the market. I have no intentions of bringing any woman into my life."

"Why? What would be so wrong with that? Do you have something against women?"

He didn't answer but continued to walk.

Rose scurried to catch up with his long-legged stride. "Or is it marriage?" she persisted. "Do you have a grudge against marriage?"

He shook his head no. "Farming is my spouse."

"That's good!" Rose reached into her small pouch and took out the tiny pen and notebook. "Can I quote you?"

"Quote me?" His face sagged into a scowl. "Is that what this is all about? Can't someone just have a conversation with you without you taking notes? Is everything anybody says going to appear in that Chicago rag you call a newspaper?"

Rose had had this conversation many times before in the course of her journalistic career. Lately, of course, in the society pages, people had been anxious to see their names in print, so possibly she was a bit rusty on her technique. She was almost a household name in Chicago. Here, she was as anonymous as the next stranger to step off the train. She needed to be vigilant.

If she was going to get people to open up to her, to learn what really drove these homesteaders—this homesteader, in particular—she'd better not be as aggressive as she was in Chicago.

One thing she had learned during her time at the *Tattler* was knowing what approach to take. Eric Johansen would need some coddling, but he seemed too smart to be flattered.

"Let's sit down here," she said, touching his elbow as she moved toward a small bench in front of the post office. "Let me start where I should—at the beginning."

He settled uneasily on the wood-slatted bench. "Start."

"I believe you know I'm a reporter with the *Chicago Tattler*. I'm here for six months doing a series of reports about homesteading." She paused and flashed him her brightest smile.

He didn't seem to be swayed, but on the other hand, he didn't get up and leave. "So what does this have to do with me?"

"I'd like to focus on one homesteader so my readers will understand this whole Dakota Territory mystique better." Rose touched the little notepad and stared directly into his eyes. "I'd like the story I write on these pages to be yours, and—"

"No!" He sprang up, his face tight. "No! Absolutely not!"

"Why not?" She stood up, a mollifying hand on his wrist.

"Simply put, I don't want to."

She hadn't faced this kind of opposition since a short stint covering the women's crime scene. Quickly her mind sought another approach. Maybe he had an ego she could appeal to. "Mr. Johansen," she purred, "you'll be the featured subject. People from across the country will read about you. You'll be famous."

"Famous." He fairly spat out the word. "I'm a farmer. I dig in the dirt for a living. Who'd want to read about me?"

She moved in for the proverbial kill. "Our subscribers. The businessmen who buy a paper from a newsboy or a newsstand. Those who pick up a discarded *Tattler* from a sidewalk or a gutter and read it. Most of them will never make it past the Mississippi, but they wonder and dream about coming out here. They want to know what your life is like. They want to live vicariously through you."

He didn't respond, and she held her breath.

So much was riding on his response. He *had* to say yes. He just had to.

Birds chirped in the early summer evening, filling the huge silence with their twitters.

The fact that he hadn't told her to leave was a promising sign, and Rose clutched at the thought.

Just as he was about to speak, a voice interrupted him. "Eric Johansen! There you are! I've been looking for you to thank you for fixing that floorboard."

A tall thin man with a shock of amazingly blond hair had come up behind them. "No thanks are necessary. By the way, Rose, this is our minister, Reverend Wilton. And, Reverend, this is Rose Kelly. She's visiting Jubilee."

The minister smiled at her. "Ah, you must be the reporter I've been hearing so much about. All of Jubilee is quite abuzz with your presence. I understand you're from Chicago?"

"Yes, I am," she said, offering her hand to the stranger. "I'm planning to be here for six months, sending a series of articles about homesteading back to my newspaper, the *Tattler*."

"What a splendid idea! Did you hear that, Eric?"

"Oh, I heard," Eric answered dryly.

Rarely does opportunity present itself on a silver platter, Rose thought, *but when it does, who am I to pass up such a gift?* She saw her chance and took it. "I'm hoping Mr. Johansen will agree to be the homesteader I feature in the series. I think he'd be perfect."

The minister rubbed his hands together. "Absolutely! Eric, don't pass it up. All of us at Redeemer will be glad to help both of you on this project. I can assure you of our support."

Eric shook his head, and Rose's heart sank.

"It would be a splendid opportunity to help Jubilee grow into a real humdinger of a town," Reverend Wilton continued. "I suspect quite a few people in Chicago read Miss Kelly's newspaper, and just imagine how many of them her articles might inspire to head out here and join us."

Eric's mouth stayed drawn in a tight, flat line.

"They could shake away the close confines of the city and come out here to experience God's love under this great blue sky." The minister's hand arced in a grand gesture over his head. "Give it some thought, Eric. I'd do it, except I'm not homesteading."

Eric sighed, and his next words gave her hope. "Reverend, I'm—"

Before he could finish his sentence, Mrs. Jenkins and the others from the church kitchen had joined them and were all chiming in with their enthusiasm for the project.

Eric didn't have a chance.

"All right, I'll do it. But with limits."

The crowd cheered, and Rose barely restrained herself from joining them.

This was going to be a glorious six months.

Thank You, she breathed. *Thank You.*

❧

Eric glared at the trees on the horizon as his horse plodded down the road. He scowled at the rabbit that ran across the road in front of him. He glowered at the hawk that swooped overhead.

What was wrong with him? Why couldn't he have just said no and been done with it? It wasn't like he had even considered being the subject of her articles. It wasn't possible. There were a million and one reasons why it wouldn't work, and every bit of him screamed out a warning: *Don't do it.*

There was only one reason why he should do it. But it was a terrible reason.

It had been a long time since his arms had held a woman. He didn't allow himself so much as to dream of love. But Rose—she'd been warm and solid and real. Suddenly his dreams seemed silly.

Too much was at risk to get involved with her scheme. He couldn't take the chance—and he certainly couldn't put his heart on the line.

But he'd made a promise, and there was no way he was going to back out on it. He'd committed himself to doing this, and he had to stay the course. He'd have to be settled with that decision.

He lifted his eyes to the cloudless sky and prayed. His petition had no words, just a sincere heartfelt appeal, and he knew God heard it.

The dirt road curved, telling him he was almost home. There was something wonderfully peaceful about that word. *Home.*

He knew every inch of it by heart, every board and nail. It was *his* house. The closest any woman had gotten to entering it was when one or two of the women from Redeemer had brought towel-wrapped dinners when he'd first begun building it, and even then, they'd only set a foot in the door.

He'd built the house himself, placing every board in the structure, every nail, every brick. It was made the way that suited him. Bookshelves lined two walls of the living room, and they were organized not by author or subject or even color, but by the date he'd read them.

There was one picture on the wall, a painting of the battle of Jericho. It had hung in his bedroom when he was a teenager, a gift from his parents right before they lost their lives from influenza, and it had hung everywhere he had lived since then.

Now, as he pulled into the yard, attended to his horse, and went inside, he saw his home in a different light.

For the first time, he noticed the dust on the table by the window. The sweat-stained kerchief tossed carelessly by the front door. His morning coffee cup still by his chair. His house was not woman-ready. She'd probably bustle in and start sweeping and dusting and cooking, and the next thing he knew, he'd have pink ruffled curtains in his kitchen.

He shuddered at the thought.

On the other hand, maybe it would be all right.

He and Rose had set boundaries for the next six months. They were simple. First, she could not shadow his every move. There was no way he could possibly get his work done if she were hanging around his neck like a clinging vine. Second, she had to respect his privacy. She was not to pry into his personal things, and snooping was definitely not allowed. Third, there would be no assumption of friendship. He was helping her out with her article, and that was the extent of it.

Eric groaned. It seemed so easy in theory, and so impossible in fact.

What *had* he done?

≈

Rose woke early the next morning and quickly dressed for church.

"There's a dinner after the service," Matthew said at the desk of the hotel. "I'm planning to get over there for at least a while."

She grinned at him. "I understand they're serving *lefse*."

He nodded. "Miss Kelly, they always serve *lefse*."

She laughed. "I imagine they do."

It seemed as if everyone in Jubilee went to Redeemer, Rose thought as she walked toward the church, joining the steady stream of people who were headed in the same direction.

Mrs. Jenkins waved at her when she entered the church and motioned her over to sit beside her. Across the room, she caught sight of the back of Eric's head, his blond hair neatly combed. Reverend Wilton was a splendid minister, and his sermon about the joys of friendship was pleasant and inspiring and buoyed her already-elated spirits even higher.

After the service, she joined the throngs of worshipers who headed for the grassy area behind the church. "We're going to eat outside," Mrs. Jenkins explained, "since it gets a bit close inside during the summer with all the folks there and the cooking going on."

She led Rose to a table where others were already seated. "Everyone, this is Rose Kelly. I'm putting her in your hands because I'm on duty at the bread table."

Her tablemates began to introduce themselves. Freya and Lars Trease, both in their midthirties, ran the store in town. Lars was as thin as Freya was thick. Linnea Gardiner was the young teacher at Jubilee's school, and Rose recalled seeing her in the *lefse*-making group at the church. Linnea's lovely blond hair curled around her face in charming tendrils. Rose sighed silently. *Linnea had the hair she'd always coveted.*

She pulled herself up short on that thought. *No, not coveted—admired. Linnea had the hair Rose had always admired.*

Thomas Pinkley was Jubilee's doctor. Arvid Frederickson

farmed north of Jubilee and usually had his wife and three children with him, but they were home with summer colds.

"I hear you're doing a story about us," Lars said. At first Rose thought he was frowning at her, but she realized that the lines over his nose were permanently etched there.

"A series of stories," Rose corrected him. "They'll certainly touch on all of you, but the main focus will be on a single homesteader."

Dr. Pinkley nodded. His silver hair and well-cut black suit made him look quite elegant. "I hear tell you'll be writing about Eric Johansen."

"That's our current plan." Rose's experience had taught her to limit what she told others when she was working on an interview but to always be ready with one question. "What can you tell me about him?"

"He's a good fellow," Lars said. "We're glad to have him in Jubilee."

"Jubilee got its start with the railroad," Linnea noted, "although it's probably a toss-up as to whether the credit for its growth should go to the railroad or the land office. People have been coming out here regularly to homestead, but there's no property left around Jubilee. It went quickly. You can't find better land than right here in the Red River Valley."

"The ground is rich and dark." Arvid dug in the grass with his toe and uncovered a patch of soil. "Look at that, Miss Kelly. You can't tell me you have earth that rich in Chicago."

The conversation was not going at all in the direction she intended, and Rose tried to steer it back.

"That's true," Rose agreed, "but I'm wondering why people would come to a place like Jubilee."

"I'm nearing retirement," the doctor said. "I wanted to finish up my medical career where I could retire and dig in the ground, plant some radishes and corn."

Freya Trease spoke next. "Lars and I came here from New York City. We had a store there, but the neighborhood started to go bad, and there was a fire, and. . ." Her eyes filled with tears, and her husband patted her hand awkwardly. She sniffed and finished, "Anyway, here we are and glad to be here."

"Me, I'm just a farmer with dirt in my bones," Arvid said. "The missus and I figured it'd be easier to coax a crop out of this river land than anywhere else, so we let Uncle Sam give us a parcel out here. All we've got to do is prove up, and with soil this rich, that shouldn't be a problem."

"What about you, Linnea?" Rose asked.

"I was in teachers' college in Rhode Island, and I'd just graduated when my parents decided to come out here, so I tagged along with them."

"These stories are so interesting," Rose said. "I think that's one of the things that drew me to newspaper writing—learning about people's lives. So you came for a variety of reasons, I see. How about Eric? Do any of you know why he came out here?"

"You could ask him," Arvid said practically, "but he might not tell you."

Rose sat up straight, all her reporter's instincts alert. "Why not?"

"Not polite."

She was baffled. Why wouldn't it be polite?

Dr. Pinkley leaned over and said in a low voice, "This is a land of new beginnings for all of us. As you've heard, each of us has our reason for coming out here."

"Aren't you curious, though?" she pressed.

He shrugged. "Not really. We all wanted a better life. Some folks were stuck in jobs that had no future. Others felt hemmed in, stuck in the middle of a city. I know at least one family came because of the grasshopper plagues in Minnesota. You've heard of those, haven't you?"

She made a face. "Yes, I have." Even in Chicago, the invasion of the hungry creatures that ate everything in their path was legendary.

"And," the doctor continued, "I suspect some left situations that couldn't be tolerated any longer. If someone wants to tell us, we'll listen, but Jubilee is all about the future. We don't revisit the past out here."

Rose couldn't have heard anything that made her more anxious to learn more. Telling her she couldn't know something just increased her curiosity.

As if on cue, Freya spotted Eric and motioned him over. "Come join us," she said when he neared the table, a heavily laden plate in his hand.

His blue eyes twinkled when he surveyed their table. "No plates? What is this, a table of sluggards? You'd better move. I've left some lefse for you, but it's going fast."

As they all stood up to go to the serving tables, Rose noticed that they had neatly maneuvered their chairs so that the only open spot was beside her.

His words came back to her, something about how the women of the church were trying to get him paired off. She couldn't resist a secret smile.

This was going to be a very interesting six months.

❧

"Wait, Mr. Johansen!" Eric turned in surprise. Nobody called him Mr. Johansen except for some of the children in town. He'd have to get her squared away on that, really fast.

He was leaving the church, his arms full of bundles of leftover food. He dropped them in his wagon and waited for Rose to catch up with him.

"I'm so glad I caught you," she panted. "I wanted to get a quick history from you before you left."

He tried not to react. "Why do you need to do that?" he asked, leaning over to pick an imaginary bit of dirt off the wheel of his wagon.

"It's common newspaper procedure," she said, a small frown marring her flawless forehead. "I was thinking I'd start with what drew you out here in the first place."

"I came here to homestead," he said. "Now I really have to be going."

He started to get in the wagon, but she stepped in front of him.

"Mr. Johansen—"

"Call me Eric. Whenever people call me Mr. Johansen, I look around for my father, and he's been with the Lord for twelve years now."

She smiled. "I see. That would startle me, too. But if you could tell me a few things about yourself, I'd certainly appreciate it."

"Miss Kelly—"

"Rose. Call me Rose. Can't you please answer a few questions? Why did you decide to leave wherever it was you lived before? What influenced you? Was it the advertisements for free land? Had you heard stories from people who'd already homesteaded?"

He knew how a trapped mouse felt—cornered, caged, and with no hope of escape. "Those are a lot of questions. You don't expect me to answer all of them, do you?" He summoned a smile—a fake one, but a smile nevertheless.

"Oh, you don't have to answer all of them. Just a few. Just one?"

"My past is not part of this," he said a bit sharply.

She tapped her foot. He couldn't help but notice it was a very small foot shod in an outrageously inappropriate style for prairie living. That pale purple leather wouldn't last a day in his farmyard.

"Just tell me a little bit. I don't like begging, but I'm going to have to do that. Please? Something?"

"No," he said. "Just no. Plain and simple no."

"Why not?"

His exasperation was edging to the point where he was going to say something awful. *God, help me out here, please. Give me the words I need.*

"I'll tell you how I chose Jubilee, but that's all."

Rose nodded. "I'll take it. Tell me the story."

"Well, there isn't really much to say. I chose it because of its name."

"You decided to come here just because this town is called Jubilee?" She looked at him disbelievingly and then took her little notepad and pen out of her purse and scribbled furiously.

He couldn't resist asking, "You know what that means, don't you?"

Rose snapped the pad shut. "Why, yes, I do, as a matter of fact. And that, my friend, makes you that much more interesting."

He watched as she marched back into the church. He'd probably done entirely the wrong thing by telling her, but maybe it was vague enough that she could use it in her story and leave his past alone.

It was true, though. A place named after the joyful forgiveness of sins and debt had to be the place for him.

How long this information would hold her was another issue. Once she started putting two and two together, this woman would come up with seven.

four

A good day's work is a noble thing. Not every day, however, is a good day to work. The soul needs nurturing the same as the body. We must feed our souls as well as our bodies.

Rose quickly found one distinction between Chicago and Jubilee. In the big city, Sunday was simply another day of the week. Life roared on as it did on the other six days. For the most part, shops were open for business, and while Rose might have had to go a bit farther to find a store that was open on Sunday, it was possible.

In Jubilee, however, things were quite different. Apparently the residents took the matter of keeping the Sabbath quite seriously. Rose stared at the CLOSED sign on Clanahan's Wagon and Livery.

"The only thing you'll find open on Sunday is the church," Matthew explained when she'd walked back to the Territorial Hotel.

"Everything else is closed?"

"Everything." The young man nodded so vigorously that his glasses slid down his nose and he had to push them back into place.

"What do I do if I have to have a wagon today?" she persisted.

"You wait unless you can borrow one from someone."

Rose leaned across the counter. "Do *you* have a wagon?"

Matthew laughed. "You go right to the point, don't you,

Miss Kelly? I'm sorry, but I don't have a wagon or even a horse. I live here in town, and I walk wherever I need to go."

"Do you know anyone who can lend me one?"

"At the risk of being impertinent," Matthew said, "is this an emergency? Can't this wait until tomorrow?"

Waiting until tomorrow was a concept to which Rose had never subscribed. Too many ideas slid into nothingness when they were forced to linger.

"I'd like to take a ride through the countryside and watch some farming in action. Remember, I'm a city girl. I know nothing about this." She smiled in what she hoped was a winning fashion.

Matthew shook his head. "You'd have to travel quite a ways. You won't find anyone in the fields today, not here in Jubilee, that is. This is a day of rest."

She nodded. "I see." She turned away from the desk and walked over the rose-patterned carpet to her room, where she sank onto her bed.

So Jubilee was closed on Sundays, was it? She liked that, even if it was inconvenient at the moment.

" 'Remember the Sabbath day, to keep it holy,' " she said aloud.

It was one of the Ten Commandments. She stood and crossed to the window. The midafternoon sun lit empty streets and shuttered stores. As far as she could see across the gloriously flat land, nothing moved—except a distant cluster of shapes. She squinted at the rebels. They were oddly shaped and seemed to be dressed in black and white.

What was this odd development in Jubilee? She stretched as far as she could and narrowed her eyes even more, until at last it all made sense.

Cows. They were cows.

She shook her head at her own silliness. She had a long, long way to go before she'd be at home here—if, in fact, that ever happened. Rose Kelly was part of the city, just as much as Eric Johansen was part of the prairie.

What was she to do with the remaining hours of her day? She reached for the leather-bound volume on top of the bureau. Maybe it was time to take another look at those commandments.

&

Monday morning broke bright and clear. Eric groaned as the first slivers of light stabbed his eyes. He hadn't slept well at all, and when he had finally fallen asleep, his dreams had been restless.

After his morning devotions—he liked to start his day with something from Proverbs—he wandered into his kitchen and remembered the lefse he'd gotten the day before.

He rolled up a piece of lefse and stuffed it into his mouth. The women had made him a basket of food after the meal yesterday. It was almost as if they didn't believe he could cook for himself. He glanced around his tiny kitchen and grimaced. They were right.

The Sunday dinners were a real boon to him. By the end of the week, though, he often found himself having to eat his own dry bread or his pitiful attempts at stew.

He splashed some water on his face and stomped out to the barn. There was never enough time to get even with farming, he thought as he mucked out the stable. His horse whinnied softly, and he rubbed its soft nose. "Yes, fellow, you're going to have some lovely hay now."

This was his favorite time of day, this time in the barn with his horse watching him with those liquid brown eyes. They'd stand beside each other, him working and the horse observing, until at last he'd turn the gray into the corral and let it graze.

"Your lazy days are about to end, my friend," he said to the horse as he evened out the straw. "Soon enough we'll be in the fields all day long, you and me. The wheat's doing well."

He led the gray out into the sunlight and paused. "Well," he asked the horse, "what do you think of Miss Rose Kelly?"

The horse shook out its mane.

"That's right. I agree. This whole thing can't come to a good end. Why did I let myself get talked into this?" He sighed and headed toward the fence on the other side, which was leaning a bit.

The gray followed him, tossing its head a bit in the sunshine.

"This is the day which the Lord hath made. I suppose it's up to me to rejoice and be glad in it, isn't it?"

The horse didn't answer but bent its elegant neck to nibble some early clover.

❧

"Tch, tch," Rose said encouragingly as she flapped the reins. The only horse Clanahan had available was Big Ole, a gigantic thing with hooves as large as dinner plates.

The wagon was as tiny as the horse was large, and as they rumbled down the road to Eric's house, she had the unwelcome thought that she was at the mercy of the beast. If he wanted to go right, then they were going right. She didn't seem to have much choice in the matter.

Eric's house was going to be easy to find, Mr. Clanahan had assured her. She was supposed to watch for a small brown house in a grove of cottonwoods. He'd also laughingly told her not to worry, that Big Ole would turn in there on his own to get a drink at the stream that ran next to Eric's house.

She looked at her surroundings as Big Ole led her along the road. Was the sky this blue over Chicago? Was it simply obscured by the black clouds that spewed forth from the smokestacks? And did the birds sing this powerfully in the city? All she could remember were the tiny sparrows and the pushy pigeons, not the songbird whose glorious melody washed over the prairie.

Her musings came to a sudden stop as Big Ole slowed his steadily clomping pace and turned in at what had to be Eric's house.

She sat in the wagon, but nobody came out. *He must be in the fields,* she thought, *but where?*

Rose gathered her skirt and carefully climbed out of the wagon. She contemplated Big Ole—should she tie him up? She laughed at the thought. If Big Ole decided to leave, there wasn't a tether in sight that could hold him.

She patted him tentatively on his haunch. "Good boy. Stay there."

"He's not a dog," Eric called from the barn door. He was wiping his hands on a cloth as he came toward her. "I see Clanahan gave you Big Ole." He ran his hand along the horse's neck. "He's a gentle giant, this one is. And reliable."

He unhooked the wagon and began to lead the horse to the pasture. "The stream winds through the pasture. He likes that stream water better than the stuff Clanahan gives him from the tank in town."

Rose had to run to keep up with his long strides. "Do you mind if we visit awhile?"

"I have work to do." His answer was short.

"I understand that. I could help you," she offered, trying to avoid the random tufts of grass that threatened her elegant little French heels.

The look he threw over his shoulder was icy. "Can you milk a cow?"

"No," Rose said brightly. "But I can learn."

He shook his head. "Perhaps another day. I have quite a bit to do, Miss Kelly, and although I've already agreed to be the subject of your articles, I still need to do my work."

"I understand. I'll be just as quiet as a mouse. You won't even know I'm here."

He let go of Big Ole's bridle, and the horse thundered happily into the pasture toward the gray that was already there, kicking up a clod of moist dirt that landed directly on her white blouse. Rose tried not to think of the stain that the soil would leave on the silk.

She knew her smile wouldn't fool him, but she tried anyway. "I've had worse things thrown on me."

His reserve melted for just a moment. "What kinds of things would a society reporter have thrown at her? Chocolates? Cakes? Champagne?"

"Ah, the three C's of fancy dinners. No, surprisingly, there have been times when people weren't glad to see me."

"That is a surprise," he said dryly.

She ignored his comment. "And I don't drink champagne. A reporter needs a clear head. Actually, I think I always need a clear head, so I stick with juice or water." Rose grinned. "But I never had any problems with chocolates or cakes."

The gray horse left Big Ole's side and came to join them, nuzzling Eric's pocket. "He wants a treat," Eric said, taking an apple out of his pocket. "Usually I wouldn't give him one so early in the day, but he'll trail after us if I don't. Right, fellow?"

"Is that his name? Fellow?"

Eric ducked his head. "He doesn't have a name."

She faced him, her hands on her hips. "Do you mean to tell me that you haven't named this beautiful animal?"

"Well, uh, you see, I—" His words stumbled out.

"I think he deserves a name." She stepped back and studied the horse. From the corner of her eye, though, she watched Eric. He hadn't smiled at all since she arrived. She couldn't stand that; she just couldn't. "You should name him something suitable, something that will make him proud."

She paused. "Something like Sir Gray Steed of the West."

That did it. He smiled, and Rose's heart soared.

"What kind of homesteader are you?" she asked.

He stopped and looked at her. "I do all right."

She shook her head. "Very funny. No, I mean do you have animals? Do you grow things?"

"I had some sheep once," he said, walking toward the barn, "but I didn't care for that."

"Why not?"

He led her into the darkness of the barn. It smelled of hay and horses—not an unpleasant smell at all. Eric pulled a pile of leather bindings from a shelf and handed them to her. "Here. Check these over for damage."

"Damage?"

"Make sure they're not coming apart."

"What am I looking for?"

"Tiny teeth marks," he answered. He picked up a burlap bag of something metal that clanked as he carried it to the barn door.

"Tiny teeth—oh. Mice. Nasty. Say, what's in that bag?" She tried not to think about what the dirty leather straps were doing to her white blouse. The spot from the dirt clod might have come out, but this pile was spelling certain doom for the fine silken fabric.

"Pieces of this and parts of that. Say, pretty soon the barn will become an oven. Come on, let's go outside to do this," he said.

"Sounds good to me." She staggered a bit under the load. It was heavier than it looked.

He moved two short stools from the side of the barn. "Have a seat."

The wind felt good on her face. She began separating the bindings and checking them over for weaknesses in the leather. "So why didn't you keep them?"

"Keep what?"

"The sheep."

"Oh, them." Eric rummaged through the burlap bag. "There should be a—oh, here it is. Well, sheep are good for two things: food and wool. Shearing sheep is quite a skill. If you don't do it well, neither you nor the sheep will come through the experience unhurt."

"Why not raise them as a food crop?"

He shook his head. "Nah. Not for me."

"I couldn't do that," she said. "Once I named them, I couldn't—"

"Named them?" For the second time that day, he laughed. "Named them? Rose, that's priceless."

She glared at him. "I don't see what's so funny about that."

"Never mind. To move on with your question, I'll tell you—this year I'm raising wheat. I tried barley once before, but it didn't do very well, so I'm sticking with wheat. By the way, it's spring wheat."

"Spring wheat is. . . ?" she asked, digging out her tiny notebook and pen from her bag, which she had attached to her waist.

"Planted in the spring. Winter wheat is planted in the winter."

"How can you plant wheat in the winter?" Her pen tore across the paper as she wrote furiously.

"It's actually planted in September, generally late in the month for better yield. I've heard winter wheat does better than spring wheat but that it's riskier since it's so cold up here during the winter, so I stick to planting spring wheat. Just about everybody up here does."

"That makes sense," Rose said, busily writing everything down in her tiny notepad. "When did you plant, by the way?"

"Well, this year I got in the fields a bit early. It was the end of April. Sometimes we don't get out there until May. It all depends on the weather." He gave a short laugh. "Everything up here depends on the weather."

"And when will it be harvested?"

"August usually. Want to see the field?" He dropped the metal components back into the bag. "I'm about ready to go for a walk."

"Sure!"

He led her to the field, and they walked along the perimeter. "See?" he said, crouching down along the edge row. "It's looking good. Strong, healthy plants, and barring any hailstorms or tornados or extended thunderstorms or plant disease, we should have a good crop this year."

She knelt beside him, ignoring the mud that was sponging up on her skirt. The entire outfit was a disaster anyway.

"The rows are about half a foot apart at minimum, although we like to give them nine inches if we can," he explained.

He stuck a finger in the dirt at the base of one of the plants and dug a small hole. "The root systems are sturdy, which helps." He covered it back up and patted the soil into place.

"Do you plant with someone else?"

"No. Why do you ask?"

"You keep saying 'we.'"

"I guess I mean God." He stood up and brushed the dirt off his hands. "Farming isn't something a man can do by himself. Each little seed is a miracle. Inside it is another plant. I can't make a seed, and I certainly can't duplicate the wondrous marvel of germination when the seed sprouts, and then when it pushes through the soil, climbing up to live under the sun."

"Well," Rose said, "you've chosen your partner wisely, then."

&

A storm was moving in with the evening shadows, and Eric built a fire to protect against the chill that came with it. Once it was crackling heartily, he pulled his chair closer to the hearth and settled in with his Bible in hand.

He needed to get squared away with this business with Rose, and he knew no better way than to take his concerns to the Lord. First he turned to his favorite passage, Psalm 23. It reminded him of the land around Jubilee.

Since he'd come out here, he'd truly been restored, just as the psalm said. The comfort of this psalm had soothed his soul many times.

He leaned back in his chair and mulled over this sudden turn his life had taken. There was no denying that Rose was a beautiful woman. Did that have anything to do with his decision to go along with her harebrained plan? Surely he had better control of himself than that. He hated to think he was so shallow that he'd follow a woman's path just because she was lovely.

Maybe it was the energy she generated. When she was near him, he felt as if he'd been placed in the middle of a tornado and swept up in its wildly churning winds.

"Speaking of winds," he said to himself as a shutter rattled wildly. The storm was arriving.

He didn't bother with a coat. The only shutter that couldn't be closed from the inside was the one in front of the house, which would take mere moments to fasten securely.

Huge raindrops plopped heavily on his shoulders as he secured the shutter. The wind whipped at his face and tore at his shirt. He made his way to the barn, fighting the wind every step of the way, and made sure everything was protected.

One thing he really needed to do was finish that storm cellar, he thought as lightning tore across the sky and thunder rumbled loudly across the fields. It was still as rudimentary as when he'd first built it.

The night sky opened, and rain poured down, drenching him to the skin. Drops were falling faster than the ground could absorb them, and the water was pooling. He ran as fast as he could back to the house.

Inside, he was glad for the fire. He got out of his wet clothes and into some dry ones, and he returned to his seat in front of the hearth—and to the subject of his earlier musings.

Rose Kelly. She was going to be snooping around his house, asking questions. That would make any man nervous.

A knock on the door broke into his musings. Who could be coming by during such a storm?

He answered the door and was surprised to see Reverend Wilton. "Come in, come in! What are you doing out in that storm?" he asked.

The minister handed Eric his wet coat. "I had dinner tonight at the Frederickson house, and I misjudged the arrival of the storm. Arvid wanted to show me his new venture."

They both smiled. Arvid Frederickson was always on the search for something new that would make his life easier. Eric thought that if Arvid would put as much effort into farming as he did in trying to get out of it, he'd be a great success. Of course, he never spoke his thoughts out loud, but from the looks he'd seen on other people's faces, he knew he wasn't alone in his theory.

"What's his new venture?"

"Ducks."

"Ducks. Ah. I see. Have a seat, Reverend, and dry off in front of the fire. I was about to have some tea. As you see, I've been out in the rain myself. Can I make you a cup, too?" Eric asked as he headed for the kitchen.

"Tea would certainly take the edge off," Reverend Wilton said. "Thank you very much."

"So Arvid's decided that ducks are the way to go, has he?" Eric called from the kitchen. "Is he planning to sell them for food, or is he interested in starting a duck egg business, or what?"

The minister waited until Eric had come back with the tea. "I'm not sure. I'm not sure that Arvid's sure. But he's got his mind set on those ducks, and he's already ordered them. They'll be arriving any day now, I guess. And who knows? Maybe they'll be just the thing, and he'll make a fortune."

"Maybe." Eric knew his single word didn't sound at all encouraging, but he knew Arvid's history.

"Say, speaking of new arrivals in town, I hear that so far

it's working out well with Miss Kelly," Reverend Wilton said.

"It depends on what you mean by 'working out well,'" Eric responded. "To be honest, Reverend, I'm uneasy about this whole business. She says she's just going to watch me work and ask questions, and she promises that I won't know she's there, but she was here today and—"

"And you knew it, didn't you?" The minister nodded understandingly. "Eric, are you concerned because she's a woman and you'd be working out here together—and often alone?"

"No!" Eric put down his mug of tea and paced across the room. "No, it's not that at all."

"Then what is it?"

Eric didn't answer at first. He looked out the window and said, "It looks like the rain is stopping. We got a good soaking, though. The wheat'll like that. And so will Arvid's ducks," he added with a wry laugh.

"You're not going to answer the question, are you?" Reverend Wilton drained the rest of his tea. "But I think you should really try to identify why you're so uneasy with Rose. She's not a bad person, you know."

"I know she isn't, but, Reverend, I could be asking the same of you."

The minister sat up, his mouth twitching as if a smile and a frown were struggling. "What do you mean by that?"

"It seems to me," Eric answered with a wink, "that there's someone in Jubilee who's got your eye."

Reverend Wilton put down his cup. "We're not here to talk about my personal life, Johansen," he said primly. "This conversation is about you—and Rose Kelly. Can you tell me why you're uncomfortable with her presence?"

Eric shook his head. "I don't know. Part of it is that—well, let's face it. Would *you* like to have somebody watching your every move?"

The minister stood up and patted Eric on the back before raising his eyes heavenward meaningfully. "I already do, Eric. I already do."

five

A friend is a valuable commodity. Companionship is important to us; without it, we shrivel as unwatered grasses in the hot sun.

Rose patted the tiny bag to make sure her paper and pen were there, gave her hair a final glance in the gilt-edged mirror, and left the hotel.

It was a glorious late June day. The sky stretched out "as infinite as God's goodness," her mother would say. Not a single cloud marred the clear blue that swept from horizon to horizon.

Pretty. Very pretty. And quiet. Very quiet.

Or was it? She stood stock-still, listening—and hearing. Beyond the immediate town, a horse clopped its way along a dirt road, its regular and slow hoofbeats muffled by the distance. A group of four crows argued about an abandoned bit of bread in the street before her. Somewhere in the houses behind the hotel, a man spoke and a woman laughed.

So much for silence!

Rose's steps led her to her first stop, the school. Linnea Gardiner knelt in front of the white-washed building, her face shaded by a large straw hat. With a soil-crusted trowel, she carefully dug a hole and then placed a tiny plant in it. Rose watched a moment before approaching her.

The young schoolteacher pushed a stray lock of blond hair

back with dirt-coated fingers. "I'm glad you stopped by."

"Don't let me interrupt your work," Rose said.

Linnea laughed. "That's one of the reasons I'm happy to see you. I need to take a break." She stood up, groaning as she rubbed the small of her back. "I think I've been in this position too long. Would you like to come in for some iced tea?"

As they entered the schoolhouse, Linnea explained that she was doing her summer sprucing up of the building and its grounds. "I do the best I can during the year, but June is my favorite time. As much as I complain, I love planting flowers. It must be because of my name—Gardiner."

"You seem to have quite the green thumb. Do you plant around your house, too?" Rose asked.

Linnea shook her head. "I don't have my own house here. Someday I hope I will." She blushed a bit. "Right now I've only got a room in the Jenkins's house, but they humor me and let me stick my blossoms in the ground there."

"Is that the Mrs. Jenkins I met at the church making *lefse*?"

"The one and the same. She's wonderful. I know I should start looking for my own place to live—maybe start a claim or maybe push a certain somebody a little harder, if you know what I mean—but the Jenkins family has become my own. I love Mr. and Mrs. Jenkins as if they were blood relatives."

Rose nodded understandingly and smiled at the schoolteacher. "So you have a fellow who's not being forthcoming?"

Linnea bent over the pitcher, but not before Rose saw a flush climb the teacher's fair cheeks. She poured them each a glass of iced tea. "Let me know what you think of it," she said. "I put some mint in it from the garden at the Jenkins's house. I think it perks it up a bit."

"It's terrific!" Rose said truthfully, taking a drink. "The mint makes it really refreshing. This is just the kind of thing a young wife should know about," she added teasingly, but Linnea looked away and said only, "Maybe."

It was time to change the subject, and Rose steered the conversation back to the matter of the flowers. "I'm impressed that you can do that and the flowers live. It must add a pleasant border to the schoolhouse."

"I hope they do. I enjoy them. But the drawback," Linnea said, sitting on the desk and staring ruefully at her hands, "is that my fingers won't be truly clean again until winter."

Rose put the glass on the desk and self-consciously tucked her hands under her tiny bag. Just a week ago she'd sat at the manicurist's at La Belle's Beauty Emporium and had her nails filed and conditioned.

The thought struck her that she wouldn't be back at La Belle's for another manicure for half a year. Her life was certainly changing.

"You're the talk of the town." Linnea's frank blue eyes met hers.

"I probably am," Rose admitted. "But within a week or two, I'll be last week's news."

Linnea grinned. "Make that a month or two. News lasts longer out here. There's not as much for it to compete with."

Rose sipped her iced tea. "How long have you lived in Jubilee?"

"Not quite two years. I came out with my family. They went back to Rhode Island last year. I stayed."

"Rhode Island is so far away. How did your family choose Jubilee?"

"Reverend Wilton's uncle was our next-door neighbor, and that's how it got started. I think I'm the only person west of the Mississippi who's from Rhode Island. Have you ever been there?"

"No, I have to admit that I haven't. What's it like?"

"It's not that much different, I guess. More water and trees. The buildings are older." Linnea chuckled. "Of course, considering that the oldest structure in Jubilee was built six years ago, there wasn't much competition."

"What do you think of Jubilee?" Rose didn't like asking so many questions. Even as a reporter, she preferred guiding people into talking to her, but this conversation with Linnea invited her questions. "Compared to Rhode Island, that is."

"I like it. The only thing that bothers me," the blond schoolteacher confessed with a surprising intensity, "is that sometimes it gets a bit lonely, especially in the summer when I'm not surrounded by the children."

"I hadn't thought of that," Rose mused aloud. "It seems like it might be even lonelier out on a farm, especially if someone was by himself, without a family to occupy him in the quiet hours. Or," she finished briskly, "maybe there aren't any quiet hours on a farm."

"There are. My parents tried homesteading, and my father said it about drove him mad to spend hours on end battling with the elements, trying to coax a living from the land. He couldn't stand that, and he couldn't stand the solitary days. One day he realized that he was so desperate for companionship that he was having a full-bore argument with himself—and losing, he claimed—and he left the plow right where it was, came back to the house, and announced, 'We're going back home.'"

"How did your mother react?"

Linnea's eyes sparkled with amusement. "She pulled out the trunks and said, 'I'm ready.' She'd never unpacked them except for the necessities."

"Interesting. I can't imagine what it must be like for those who are homesteading and living by themselves." She swirled the iced tea innocently.

"You mean like Eric?" Linnea smiled impishly. "I wondered when you'd ask about him again."

An uneasy blush began its telltale climb up Rose's throat, and she shook her head adamantly. "He's just the subject of my articles for the *Tattler*. I thought he'd be a good choice since he is alone. I find that intriguing."

"I'm sure you do," Linnea teased. "Actually, we all do. He's quite handsome, in a farming sort of way."

" 'A farming sort of way'? What do you mean?"

Linnea shook her head. "I've discovered that God put the land in some people's hearts. It's not in mine, but it is in Eric's. Part of Eric *is* Dakota. He belongs here on the land, digging in it. My digging is limited to gardens in town. Eric, though, he's planting his own roots, and they're going deep down into the ground."

Rose said good-bye to Linnea, promising to see her again soon, and left the schoolhouse, her head spinning with what she'd learned. None of this was what she'd supposed it would be, not a bit of it. She'd always hoped one of her stories would change someone's life. She'd never expected that life to be hers.

Linnea was one of the surprises. In Chicago, Rose had many acquaintances who wanted to see her, wanted to be around her, wanted to share their lives with her. But none of them, she now realized, were friends, and the hole in her life was now gaping.

When she'd talked to the schoolteacher, she felt an immediate bond that settled into her soul. She'd never really had a best friend to share confidences and laughter with, and her short time with Linnea made her hunger for that.

She straightened her stance, lifted her chin, and began to walk briskly. This was a silly, melodramatic train of thought, and it was over. If she didn't guard her thoughts better, she'd be dreaming of falling in love while she was in Jubilee, and that, she told herself, was absurd.

She'd never fall in love with Eric.

Who said anything about Eric? the silent voice asked. She couldn't stop the smile that curved her lips dreamily.

She might not make it through these six months if she didn't rein in her imagination. Becoming friends with Linnea was one thing. Falling in love with Eric was something else entirely.

With determination, she hitched her little bag closer and headed for her next stop, the mercantile. It was right in the center of the town, across from the bank. Even this early, Jubilee was settling into a traditional city structure.

After the brightness of daylight, the interior of the store was dark. The matter wasn't helped at all with the mounds of goods in the single window, blocking out most of the light. Rose blinked several times to get her bearings.

When her eyes became accustomed to the dim interior, she realized that this was nothing like the large stores she shopped at in Chicago. The small room was crammed with objects of all sizes, shapes, and hues. A table in the center of the store was piled with bolts of fabric. Vivid red calico, deep blue poplin, coffee-brown chambray, and delicate pink lawn created a kaleidoscope of color.

Barrels, boxes, cartons, and jars vied for room and were stacked on top of each other in precarious pyramids.

Over it all, the smells—pickles, flour, soap, oil, fish—blended into one.

"Miss Kelly!" Freya Trease rose, laboriously from her seat

behind the counter, her ample figure swathed in a green sprigged apron. "It's good to see you again."

"Please call me Rose. This is a wonderful store."

"Thank you." Freya brushed an invisible speck from her voluminous bodice. "It's probably quite different from what you're used to in the big city."

"We have small stores, too." Rose picked up a roll of white lace and studied it. "This would be lovely as an edging, wouldn't it?"

"It would," Freya agreed. "Is there something in particular you're looking for?"

Rose put back the spool of lace. "Not today, but I know I will eventually. After all, I'm here for six months."

"Six months can be a lifetime, or it can pass in the blink of an eye." The plump shopkeeper wiped the counter with a cloth she pulled from her apron pocket. "This land will be the death of me yet."

This was exactly the kind of thing she was looking for. Although the focus of her articles would be the home-steader, insights into the lives of those who shared his community would make the stories come alive.

"Why do you say that?" she asked, trying to appear casual as she ran her hand over the edge of the pickle barrel.

"The dust from the fields," Freya said, showing Rose the smudged cloth. "But it's not as bad as during harvest."

"So living here is a real trial, is it?" Rose suggested, hoping that Freya would disagree—and provide her with a quotable line.

"It can be. The mosquitoes in summer, the blizzards and biting cold in winter—yes, there are times when I think that I was out of my mind to leave New York."

"Why do you stay? Because of the store? Your husband?"

Freya smiled. "I stay because this is the most beautiful place on earth."

Rose glanced out the window at the building across the street. The rough-hewn exterior was a marked contrast to the elegant sign grandly proclaiming it to be HOMESTEAD HONESTY BANK in black and gold script.

Beautiful? She'd heard that beauty was in the eye of the beholder, but there had to be something terribly wrong with Freya's eyes.

The shopkeeper laughed. "You don't believe me, do you?" She shrugged her well-padded shoulders and looked Rose directly in the eyes. "This is the perfect place for some people but not for everyone. We all have our own reward waiting for us, our final home, but I've found that God has settled us differently on earth. My ideal home may not be yours."

Rose knew where her ideal home was—her roomy apartment overlooking the crowded skyline of Chicago. The city teemed with life. Even though she'd just arrived in Jubilee, she knew she could never stay here.

The image of Eric Johansen floated into her mind, and she immediately corrected herself: She *could* stay here. Maybe.

"What do you know about Mr. Johansen?" she asked Freya, trying to make her words sound like an idle question. "He seems to be happy here."

Freya's face clouded. "He is. There's something holding on to him, though."

"Really? Why, I wonder what it could be."

"I don't know." The dust cloth snapped once more across the spotless counter and disappeared back into the roomy apron. "It's not my business."

Unspoken, the sentence continued, *And it's not yours, either.*

Experience had taught her to listen to what was not said, and Freya's comment increased Rose's curiosity. The shopkeeper didn't seem to know what dark event marked Eric's history, but the fact that she had sensed it was important.

Discovering a delicious tidbit like something mysterious in Eric's past was enough to add a spring to her step. She was like a bloodhound on the track of an enticing scent, and it led her right to the person of Eric Johansen himself.

≈

Eric shut his Bible. There was something about reading the Word that reached into his soul and calmed him. Lately he'd found himself turning to it more for the comfort it offered him.

This was his fourth summer in Jubilee. His body was already tuned to the flow of nature in the territory, to the growing seasons that echoed his own. June was the month of new life. He'd come to anticipate this time when the earth burst into glorious green.

But now, instead of feeling great anticipation, he was unsettled.

What had he agreed to? Had he really said he'd allow Rose Kelly to follow him around?

He snorted. Fool woman. She'd probably break her ankle in a gopher hole or pass out from sunstroke or get bitten by a rabid skunk.

Or, he realized as he rose to his feet, those things would happen to him as he chased around after her, trying to save her. He'd be lucky to make it through these six months in one piece.

Enough complaining. He had some ducklings to pick up. Arvid had gotten to him, and in sympathy, he'd agreed to take a few ducklings. If he didn't get moving, they'd be full-grown ducks by the time he got there.

There was never enough time in the day, not in June. But he wasn't going to whimper and cry about that. He'd rather be busy. There was only so much time a man could spend with his thoughts.

The sun warmed the air, and he dropped his jacket back on the hook inside the door. He wouldn't need it.

"This is the day that the Lord hath made; let us rejoice and be glad in it."

The Good Book certainly had that right!

❧

"Go down that road until you see the cottonwood with the bent trunk. Take a right. After a while, you'll see a granite rock on the left. Go a mile or so past that. The road curves a bit, and then it'll fork. Head left, and the first farm on the right is Arvid's. You can't miss it."

Matthew pushed across the counter the scrap of paper on which he had sketched the way to Arvid Frederickson's farm.

Rose took it and stared at it. It seemed simple enough. She'd been in Jubilee for two weeks, and she was finally feeling comfortable with the prairie town.

But after half an hour of driving the small wagon down country roads that all looked the same, she had to admit that she had no earthly idea where she was.

This land was so flat, she should have been able to see all the way to Omaha. But there were deceptive dips and curves in the earth, and no matter how she looked, or which road she went down, she didn't see anything that looked remotely like a farm.

Finally, in desperation, she stopped the huge horse and

climbed up on the seat of the wagon. Big Ole snorted and pawed at the ground, and the ramshackle wagon shimmied. She stood atop the wooden plank bench like a tottering sentinel on the prairie, scanning the horizon for a recognizable sign.

She saw something in the distance, a tiny squarish spot. Carefully she gathered her skirts and prepared to climb down when she realized the faraway spot was moving. It wasn't a farm, but someone else with a wagon. Whoever it was didn't seem to be far away. She'd just wait.

The little spot moved slowly toward her, inching across the landscape. She frowned at it. At this rate, it would be Independence Day before it got to her. Luckily she had her little bag with her. She could make use of this time and record her thoughts so far. Her first story was due in a few days, and she had the perfect angle for it. She took out the pad and pen and began to write. Within minutes her pen was racing across the paper, and she was engrossed in her story.

"Miss Kelly?" Eric's voice spoke right beside her, and her pen scratched a wild line across the sheet.

"You shouldn't sneak up on a body. You almost gave me heart failure!" She put her hand on her chest, and even through the thick cotton weave of her suit, she could feel the pounding.

"I'm sorry." His apology was tinged with amusement, and she glared at him.

"You don't sound sorry."

Big Ole shifted uneasily, and Eric moved quickly to his side. "Shhh, boy," he soothed. "Shhh." He looked at Rose. "I didn't mean to startle you," he said, his hand still protectively on Big Ole's bridle. "But it's not often people just pull over to the side of the road out here and scribble out a few words."

Now that her heart had returned to its normal beating, she remembered her earlier mission. "I wasn't scribbling, I was writing. And I'm out here because I'm lost."

"How could you be—" he began, and then he stopped. "Oh, never mind. Where did you intend to go?"

"I was on my way to Arvid's farm."

"Arvid?" He shook his head in disbelief. "Why would you want to go out there?"

"I'm interviewing him."

"I thought you were interviewing me."

She put the notepad back in her purse. Then she tucked the tiny pen in there, too. With great deliberation, she closed the bag, then faced him. "I tried to, Eric. I really did. I got one thing. One thing."

Eric's extraordinary silence about his past was aggravating her irrationally. She could write the article—and, in fact, she just had—without that information, but not knowing was driving her out of her mind. He was so adamant about not telling her that she was determined he was going to do it.

"Can you direct me to Mr. Frederickson's farm, please?" she asked primly. "I have a few questions for the gentleman." She lifted her chin. "If you won't talk to me, perhaps he will."

six

*When the land is this vast, we try to tether ourselves
in place by creating a web with others. It is not enough
to do this and call it done. Our lives always need to be
tended as if they were growing things, because they are,
in fact, just that.*

This wasn't what Eric wanted to hear. He wanted to pick
up his ducklings and be on his way back home. But if he
led Rose to Arvid's farm, it wouldn't be that simple. They'd
end up talking about the day's weather, and then Arvid
would take him out to the pond to look at the ducks,
and after that they'd take a look at the fields and check on
the seedlings, and the next thing he knew, they'd all be sitting
around the kitchen table drinking Arvid's Norwegian coffee
and eating his cinnamon cookies.

All he wanted were his ducks.

But there was no way around it. He was going to Arvid's,
and so was she. The only consolation he could find in the
matter was that they'd be in separate wagons on the way out.

He didn't dare leave her alone with Arvid. Who knew
what the man would tell Rose? Arvid wasn't the kind of
fellow to let a little lack of knowledge stand in his way. He'd
have a story of some kind to tell Rose.

"Just follow me," he said, trying not to sound as if he were
begrudging her anything.

"I don't want to take you out of your way," she answered,

but her relief was clear in her tone. "You could point me in the right direction and—"

He couldn't resist smiling. "Seems to me you were already pointed in the right direction and it didn't do you a bit of good."

She grinned back ruefully. "You know, with a landscape as open as this, you wouldn't think I'd miss something like a tree or a rock or another road." She touched his arm, and his breath caught as he saw again how tiny her hand was. She was such a city woman, so delicate and fragile.

With an effort, he brought himself back to the conversation. "If it's any comfort, you're not far from his farm."

Big Ole snorted impatiently and shook his mane, and Eric nodded at him. "We'd better go before Big Ole takes you back to Jubilee."

Arvid was standing in his yard when they pulled up. "Well, well, well," he said, coming to greet them both. "Two for the price of one, I guess."

"As it turns out, we were both coming out here to see you." Rose leaped out of the wagon before Eric could help her. "But I was lost."

"Lost?" Arvid's eyes twinkled with amusement. "Out here?"

"One of these days," she said, "you'll have signposts all along these roads. Mark my words."

The farmer roared and shook his head. "One of these days a long time from now, maybe. You stay here long enough, it'll be second nature to you, knowing when to turn on these roads."

"I'll just be here six months. And then it's back to Chicago, land of street signs and lampposts."

A knife twisted in Eric's chest. *Six months.* He didn't know if he wanted her to go—or stay. She was changing things in his life, and he didn't like it. He had carefully built a life that was solitary. Jubilee had been the perfect place for him to do that, too. It had allowed him to hide within the life he created for himself. And now in these short two weeks, she had begun to tear down those self-made barriers and force him to think about emotions he'd tucked away long ago.

"Can I pick up the ducklings?" he asked abruptly.

"Sure," Arvid said. "Miss Kelly, you might like to see this."

As they walked toward Arvid's barn, he explained, "Some folks here are raising chickens, but I thought I'd give ducks a try. I'm not sure how it's going to work out, but we'll see. I've got some little fellows set aside for Eric."

The barn still held the morning's coolness, and sunlight filtered through the open door. Bits of dust and straw floated in the air like speckled gold.

Eric heard the ducklings before he saw them. "I've got a box for—" he began, but Rose interrupted him.

"These are the sweetest creatures on the earth," she said, picking one up and cradling it in her hands. "Eric, they'll be wonderful pets."

Eric and Arvid exchanged glances, and Eric cleared his throat. "Uh, Rose, I don't—"

"Just look at this face." She held it close to his chest. "Look at it. What a beautiful little thing God has made. Can I name it? Just this one?"

"Rose—"

"Please?" she wheedled. "I have the perfect name for him. I want to call him Downy."

"Downy the Duck." Arvid's voice sounded suspiciously like he was trying to choke back a laugh, and Eric groaned. He'd give this story half a day before it was all over Jubilee.

"Shhh!" he hissed to Arvid. "You're not making this any easier."

"Making what easier?" Rose's face was soft with love as she kissed the duckling on the head. He'd have to avoid looking into those moss-green eyes if he were ever to have control over his emotions.

Eric sighed. "Nothing. Downy it is."

❧

Rose tapped her fingers on the desk in her room at the Territorial. In the distance, random bangs and snaps told her that boys were shooting off leftover firecrackers. Independence Day had been quite the celebration in Jubilee, complete with a program of music, drama, and oration. She and Linnea had feasted on freshly squeezed lemonade and sampled trays of cookies and cakes and dessert breads.

It was wonderful fodder for her articles. She'd left the big city to find the true America. George would love the angle. It was that ability to tap into the likes of the reading public that had made him such a good editor at the *Tattler.*

She needed to get moving on the articles about Eric, though. She'd go out to his farm bright and early the next day and ask him directly. And if she didn't get good answers from him, she'd move into investigative reporting mode.

There was something she didn't know about him, and it was eating at her not only because as a reporter she was trained to ferret out more information than she'd use in her writing, but also because she had to find out what had carved those two little lines over his nose. Some sorrow, some worry, perhaps even some sin had put those deep etchings there, and if she was going to invest her heart, she wanted to know why.

She rubbed her eyes and leaned back. She must need

sleep to be thinking like that. He was the subject of her articles and no more.

As soon as the sun came up the next day, she'd confront him directly.

But opportunity changed her plans.

Matthew was at the desk of the Territorial the next morning, his eyes looking as tired as hers felt. "I came in early," he explained, "since a skunk decided to nest under the steps of my house. It surprised me, and I surprised it, and I'm sure you can smell the result. I've done all I can to get the smell out, and I apologize if I haven't—"

She held up her hand to stop the cascade of words. "Not a problem. You smell fine." It wasn't much of an untruth. He had doused himself with something flowery and strong that did a fairly good job of disguising the remnants of the run-in with the skunk.

"Are you going out, Miss Kelly?" Matthew rubbed his eyes and yawned.

"Soon. I'm going to Eric Johansen's farm."

Matthew smiled. "He's a nice fellow. I'll be looking forward to reading your stories about him."

"Thank you." She leaned in a bit closer, and the skunk odor grew stronger. "Say, I wonder if you can help me."

"I'd be glad to, Miss Kelly. What can I do?"

"I didn't get where Eric came here from. Do you know where he lived before he moved to Jubilee?"

"I'm sorry," Matthew said, "but I don't. Not exactly, that is. East, I suppose. Everybody came from the East, I think."

"Do you have any idea what he did before he got here? Was he a teacher?"

Matthew shook his head. "A teacher? No, I don't think so."

She took a deep breath. "He's a good man, isn't he? I

mean, he hasn't been in prison?"

"Prison?" Matthew gaped at her. "What on earth would give you that idea? Prison? No. Not Mr. Johansen. There's not a squarer man in Jubilee than him."

Rose nodded. "I see. That's what I thought. Thank you, Matthew. That's just what I needed to know."

Or not, she thought as she left. She'd come away with basically no more information than she'd started with.

"Miss Kelly!" Mrs. Jenkins waved at her from across the street and hurried to join Rose in front of the Territorial. "What are you doing out so early?" she asked breathlessly.

"I'm going to Eric Johansen's farm."

Mrs. Jenkins beamed at her. "How's that progressing? You must be getting splendid material for your articles from him."

"I am," Rose began and then stopped. She could hear her editor's voice as clearly as if he were speaking in her ear. *Seize the moment, Kelly. Use what's given you, and if it's not given to you, go out and get it and take it. But keep it honest, and keep it clean.* Well, this was honest—and fairly clean. "It's quite interesting, but I'm having trouble getting background from him." She winked conspiratorially at Mrs. Jenkins. "You know how men are. They just will not talk about themselves."

"What do you need to know?"

"Where he lived before he moved to Jubilee. What he did for a living. That kind of thing."

Mrs. Jenkins tilted her head thoughtfully, her white hair catching the early sunshine. "Now isn't that odd? I don't have a clue."

"I'm sure it's all perfectly legitimate," Rose assured her, "but it does make me wonder a bit. After all, it's not like he was a criminal, I'm sure."

It was amazing how many people were out and about at this time of day. Within an hour, Rose had visited with almost everyone she'd met in Jubilee. After Mrs. Jenkins, she saw Arvid, then Linnea, who didn't have much time to talk as she was on her way to the church to check on some new candlesticks, and even the Treases as they opened their store for the day. Each person had the same answer to her questions.

No one knew about Eric Johansen's past.

She'd planted her own kind of seeds during her morning stroll, and if they didn't bear fruit fairly soon—perhaps that was an answer in itself.

❧

Eric walked through his wheat field, appraising the tiny clusters at the end of the stalks. This would be a good yield if the weather held. Of course, hail, rain, drought, even insects could change everything.

And to think this had all come from a bag of tiny seeds. What a miracle!

"How does it look?"

Her voice startled him, and he stood up so quickly that his head spun.

"Good so far. I'm hoping for a bountiful crop, but we still have a ways to go before we can count on the harvest."

The hem of her skirt moved, and a tiny beak peeked out to nab an unsuspecting beetle. "You have company, I see," he commented dryly.

"Company?" she asked blankly.

"The ducks." He pointed at her feet, where one of the ducks was now pecking at her shoelace.

"I must not have shut the gate," she said as she knelt and gathered the ducklings in her arms. "I'll take them back."

There were more than she could hold, and as soon as she captured one, another would wriggle free. "You hold those two," he told her, "and I'll get the rest of them."

"You won't even know I'm there," he thought to himself as one of the ducks veered off under the wheat and he had to leap the row to catch it. *"I'll be a quiet little shadow,"* or *whatever it was you said. Ha.*

At last they had the ducks safely in their arms and then back in the pen. The creatures were usually all right when he was around, but he liked to keep them in their cage when he was out in the field.

"Downy's quite the leader, isn't he?" Rose asked proudly as Eric latched the ducklings' pen.

"If he were human, he'd be running for governor, I'm sure." Eric stood, and she followed suit. "Are you planning on spending the day out here?"

Rose frowned at him. "Well, that wasn't exactly the most gracious invitation."

He jammed his hands inside his pockets and felt his fingers clench into fists. This was going all wrong. Whenever he was around Rose, his social graces tumbled to rock bottom. He felt like a gawky teenager around the belle of the town.

He summoned all the poise he could muster. "I'm sorry. I didn't mean to be so rude. What did you need from me today? Did you want to learn more about wheat? The operation of the farm? Perhaps a bit about the Homestead Act?"

"No," she said simply. "I want to learn more about you."

"Ah."

"I want to know about your life before Jubilee, where you lived, what you did for a living. Who were your parents, and do you have brothers and sisters? Did you have a dog when you were a boy? What did you read? What were your dreams?"

He took a breath. "My parents are both deceased. I have no brothers or sisters, and I didn't have a dog."

"Tell me more, Eric. Let me know you." She leaned closer, and his breath caught in his throat.

With an effort, he pushed away the thought of taking her in his arms. "There is no more."

She put her hand on his arm. "Eric, are you running away from something?"

He swallowed. "Aren't we all?" he answered lightly. "Now I really have to get back to work."

"Eric. . ." She followed him as he started to walk back to the fields, and he stopped.

Without turning around, he said, "Rose, we made a pact when I said I'd be the subject of your articles. Do you remember the three terms of our agreement?"

"I can't shadow you. I have to respect your privacy. There is no assumption of friendship." Had he imagined it, or had her voice cracked on the last sentence?

"Quit asking about my past. Just quit," he said. "It has nothing to do with my homesteading, and thus nothing to do with you or your articles. Leave it alone. Leave me alone."

He strode into his fields, wondering why he felt as if his world had just crashed down around him—again.

ð

Rose walked through the twilight and looked at the houses in Jubilee. They weren't all that different from the ones in Chicago, she told herself. Inside each one, people lived, people with the same wants and needs as those in the city.

They needed food and water and shelter to keep their bodies alive and healthy. And they needed God to keep their souls alive and healthy. Jubilee wasn't a rough-and-tumble wild town. Quite the contrary—a sense of moral strength was evident in the residents, a trust in a higher power that came through in their everyday lives.

She was changing, too, she realized. She'd lost some of the edge she'd had, and she honestly didn't know if she wanted it back. When she'd held that duckling and it had settled trustingly into her hands, she'd felt something shift inside her—felt it settle and make a home.

Children's laughter floated from one of the houses, and a pang struck her heart. Suddenly she was tired, very tired, of living like a whirlwind in Chicago. She wanted to slow down, to feel earth beneath her feet rather than the sidewalks of the city. There was more to life than the run of parties she covered for the *Tattler*.

Her walk had taken her through the circuit of the small town and brought her back to the center. She was just about to return to the room at the Territorial when Linnea caught up to her.

"Rose," the schoolteacher said breathlessly, "you certainly do walk briskly. I've been trying to catch up with you since the corner."

Her pace hadn't seemed rapid to her, but she was still moving at the speed of the city, where everything went faster. "Sorry," she apologized. "I was thinking. I could use a rest now, though. Let's sit here." She motioned toward the bench across from the church.

"How are you liking Jubilee so far?" Linnea asked when they had seated themselves.

The evening had deepened since Rose had begun her walk, and she looked down the street at the darkening town. "I like it," she said simply at last. "I do."

"It's a splendid place to live, you know," Linnea said. "We chose to live here, and you'll have to excuse us if we're a bit protective of our own."

Rose's head swung around, and she stared at Linnea. "What on earth do you mean? Are you saying that I've done something wrong here?" Her breath stalled in her throat. Quickly she reviewed her activities since arriving. What could she have said or done that would have offended the residents of Jubilee?

"It seems as if almost everyone here is talking about your visit."

Rose struggled to put the words together so they would make sense. What was Linnea talking about?

The icy edge to Linnea's voice struck fear into Rose's heart. She needed the cooperation of the townspeople for her stories to succeed. Had she alienated them already?

Even in the cool of the summer evening, she began to sweat. She needed their help.

Eric lives here, too, she reminded herself. *Rose Kelly, if you've driven him away, you have nothing. Was that why he was so standoffish today? Oh, dear God, help me. Please help.*

She took a deep breath and spoke. Her voice was remarkably steady and strong. "Linnea, what aren't you telling me? What do I need to know that I don't?"

Linnea didn't meet her gaze for a moment, and when she finally faced Rose, her face was filled with pain. "When you arrived in Jubilee, I was at the station. You were so elegant, so exciting, and I thought—I thought you might be my friend." Tears clouded her usually clear eyes. "But I didn't expect that you would do that."

"Do what?" She knew she sounded snappish, but she couldn't help it. If Linnea had a problem, why didn't she just say so? This sashaying around the lamppost was frustrating.

A single tear spilled over and coursed down Linnea's pale cheek. "Under the guise of friendship, you were researching your stories, trying to make us talk about Eric. Every single conversation that we had was directed toward your articles. Did we even matter to you?"

Rose started to speak, but Linnea interrupted her. "And it wasn't just that. You wouldn't stop digging, trying to find something horrible in Eric's past. Even when we said you shouldn't, you kept on. Why can't you just leave him alone?"

"I was not—" Rose began, but even as she spoke, she knew she had done just that. Now that she looked back on what she'd said earlier in the day to each person she'd talked to, the innuendos she'd planted, she realized how manipulative she'd been.

"Did you really think we'd talk behind his back?" Linnea shook her head sadly. "We would never do that. Never."

"I was only trying to find out more about him," Rose protested. "Secondary interviews are an accepted form of newspaper work."

For a moment, Linnea didn't say anything. Then she said with a touch of resignation in her voice, "That may be true in Chicago, but things are different in Jubilee. What you might call 'investigation' is what we'd consider 'prying.' To be honest, people are feeling as if you've taken advantage of their goodwill."

This wasn't the first time someone had accused Rose of snooping to get information, but the charge hadn't bothered her before.

"I'm sorry. I really am." The words were true. She hadn't intended to hurt anyone. "I wanted to fill in the spaces in

Eric's history—and there are some major gaps there, you know."

Linnea seemed to relent a bit. "You can't do that."

"I can't?" She tried not to show how those words sparked her interest anew. "Why not?"

The schoolteacher shook her head. "Rose, don't ask."

"I just wonder where he was before he came here. Did he ever tell you?"

"Who knows? It's not like he'd ever say—or we would ever ask."

"Why not?" For the life of her, she'd never understand this town's ability to overlook the past.

"It's just the way we are," Linnea said. "One day, I hope you'll understand."

Rose stood up. She'd respect it, but she'd never understand it.

☙

Eric herded the ducklings into the cage he'd built for them beside the barn. They were the silliest creatures he'd ever seen. As soon as he thought he had them corralled, one would waddle out, and the others would follow.

He rocked back on his heels and watched the ducks. One of them seemed to be the ringleader. It didn't surprise him that it was the one Rose had named Downy.

How had this woman finagled her way into his life. . .and his heart? He couldn't quite trust her, but more than that, he couldn't quite *not* trust her. It was as if his heart had its own mind.

He thought back to the way her face had softened as she held Downy. He'd known at that moment that she wasn't just a big-city newspaperwoman with hard edges. He saw intelligence compliment her inquisitiveness, and tenderness temper her crustiness. She was quite a woman.

He looked out toward his fields. The moonlight was bright on the newly emerging wheat, and he thought he'd never seen anything as beautiful as this field on this night.

A duckling quacked beside him, and he moved protectively closer to the cage as something rustled in the tall grass next to the barn. He smiled as he remembered Rose holding Downy. The glossy veneer of her big-city ways had vanished when she had the soft duckling in her hands.

Only a city girl would name something destined for the dinner table. Downy nipped his trouser leg through the cage, and Eric chuckled. "Don't worry. You're safe. Thanks to a pushy newspaperwoman from Chicago who can't keep her nose out of my business, you'll live a nice full life here."

He stroked Downy's soft head through the grating of the cage. It was a beautiful night. Nothing on earth could compare to a July night with moonlight spilling across the land.

God had given him his share of problems, his share of suffering, but He'd also given him a full portion of blessings. Tonight his plate was full.

July was the month of beginnings, a time of tender green shoots, of precious ducklings, of strange newspaperwomen who came and tore your life apart.

≥

As Rose went into Redeemer Church, the atmosphere wasn't quite as frosty. People nodded to her, perhaps not as amiably as before, but they were at least recognizing her.

She sat in the front row of the church, her Bible positioned primly on her knees. This morning she'd taken special care with her appearance, and her sleek reddish-gold hair was pulled back into a tight bun with a new white lace bow riding atop it.

Her dress, a pale blue and white windowpane check, was new, having been fashioned just this week by Mrs. Jenkins, who, she'd found out, had sewing talents equal to those she had in the kitchen.

Linnea, who sat at the other end of the pew, nodded briefly to her before turning her eyes back to Reverend Wilton, who was approaching the front of the church. Linnea's eyes looked as red as Rose's felt.

After a mostly sleepless night, she'd come to the decision that she couldn't worry too much about the townspeople mistrusting her. She had asked the questions she'd had to ask. There was no more she could do.

Reverend Wilton began the service, and she opened her Bible to the day's text, which, according to the sign at the side of the sanctuary, was Proverbs 18:4–8. As the minister read the Scripture aloud, she followed along with a growing sense of distress. " 'A fool's mouth is his destruction,' " read Reverend Wilton.

She could feel the congregation's eyes on her, blaming, accusing. And in the back of her mind, she heard her mother's tired voice: *"Rose, dear, watch your words. Take your time. Think before you speak."*

Rose bent her head as the minister led the congregation in silent prayer.

God had given her this impetuous mouth. Could He also give her the power to control it?

seven

Inside each of us is a big locked room with double-bolted cabinets and closets where we hide our sins not from others as much as from ourselves. We may not see those sinful blots on our souls, but they remain there, hidden away and carefully caged, always hoping for the day when they can wriggle free.

Rose sat in her tidy room at the Territorial, her little note-pad open beside her. She scowled at it and tapped her pen testily. For the most part, the sheets of paper were empty.

She had a story due in the mail by the end of the day, and she was no further along than she'd been when she first arrived.

Where to start? She stood up and paced across the room, the rhythm of her steps helping her direct her unfocused thoughts.

She had many possible angles to take on the story. Mentally she sorted through them, trying to determine which was the best.

George Marshall, her editor at the *Tattler*, had given her some wonderful advice when she'd begun writing for the newspaper. She imagined him standing beside her, clucking in dismay at her skimpy notes. *"Don't know where to start? How about the beginning?"*

She sat down, and slowly, at first, but with increasing speed, she began to tell the tale of her arrival in Jubilee, carefully leaving out her first unexpected meeting with Eric Johansen. This was Jubilee's story.

At last she had it ready. Woven into it were the notes she'd taken so far. She read it through one more time and sat back in her chair, smiling with satisfaction. It was good, and her readers would love it.

She gathered up the story and her little bag and left to send the story.

The small wooden building in the center of the town housed both the telegraph office and the post office. It hummed with activity, and she had to stand in line at the counter.

She wasn't intentionally eavesdropping, but the building was so tiny and crowded that hearing others' conversations was unavoidable. Years of training in the newspaper business had made it nearly impossible for her not to pay attention to those speaking around her.

Two men in work clothes discussed the progress of their respective crops. A woman with two children playing tag around her ankles talked to an older woman about a laundry mishap. An older couple exchanged brief comments about the possibility of rain.

At last it was her turn, and the young man behind the counter, who couldn't have been older than seventeen, put down the mail he was sorting and took the envelope from her. "Chicago, eh?" he asked. "Is this one of those articles I've been hearing so much about?"

All discussions in the room ceased, and an almost-palpable silence fell over the crowd. Everyone turned and stared at her.

Rose smiled widely at all of them. "Why, yes it is, and I imagine you're all curious about what it says, aren't you?"

The assembled townspeople murmured in assent.

"I'll be delighted to share it with you when it goes into print, which should be soon. My editor at the *Tattler* has promised to send me copies. I hope you'll all be pleased with what I've written."

A slow current of excitement ran through the group, and relief washed through her veins. Perhaps the veil of suspicion had been lifted.

As she turned to leave, she noticed the top envelope of the pile that the mail clerk had been holding. The address brought her up short.

Dr. Eric Johansen.

After that, *Boston Hospital* had been crossed out and *Jubilee, Dakota Territory*, added.

Doctor? Eric was a doctor?

Why would a man leave a medical career in Boston and come to Dakota—and not practice medicine?

And furthermore, why wouldn't he just tell her that?

&

Eric checked his reflection in the cracked mirror that hung in his bedroom. He looked presentable enough. He must be losing his edge, letting the people at church talk him into this.

A play. And a comic romance, too.

True, he wasn't portraying the lead character, a young swain who, through a series of misunderstandings, ended up courting his loved one's pig.

It could have been worse, he reminded himself. He could have been cast as the pig.

He rode into town, reviewing his lines. He was portraying the next-door neighbor in the play, and although he didn't have many lines, he'd never acted before. He must be out of his mind. That was the only rational explanation.

The play was being staged in the town hall, Jubilee's newest addition. A cluster of people were already milling around the door, waiting for the play to begin. Eric slipped past the group and made it to the back room, where the cast was getting ready.

The cast members were nervously reviewing their lines as if they were opening in New York City. The atmosphere was charged with anticipation.

Eric donned a formal black coat for his part in the play, then wandered through the packed room. Although the play featured only six roles, with the addition of the director, the costumer, and the prompter, the room quickly became overly humid and extremely hot. He ducked outside, welcoming the cool night air.

"You're going to the play, too?" Rose's voice came out of the shadows.

"I'm in the play."

"Ah, a new career for Eric Johansen?"

He froze. Something in her tone made him wonder what she had heard, what she knew—or thought she knew.

"Tonight is my debut and my swan song," he answered lightly. "I suspect after this performance, I won't be called on again to act."

"You never know," she said, moving toward him. "You may have hidden talents."

That did it.

"It's nearly curtain time. I'd better head back inside." Before she could say more, he darted back into the building.

Somehow, in a corner of the busy back room, he found a pocket of solitude. *God, I need Your guidance more than ever. I thought I was getting away from all my mistakes by coming here, but apparently I brought my past with me. And now Rose is here, and without Your help, I'm afraid I might fall in love with her. I can't do that. Help me know what to do. I need You more than ever. I'm lost. . .again.*

❧

The play was charming, Rose thought. It wasn't anything that would have made the dramatic circles in Chicago, but it was entertaining. And while Eric would never be the darling of the Broadway stage, he'd done a respectable job with his role.

"Now don't forget about that concert next week," Mrs. Jenkins said as they left the town hall. "Charlotta Allen is quite the rage in New York City, and we're very lucky to get her to perform here."

Rose had no idea who Charlotta Allen was, and she was fairly sure that she would have come across the name in her work with the *Tattler* if the woman had been famous in New York. Nevertheless, she looked forward to the opportunity to hear her.

The evening had been quite revealing, all in all. Apparently Jubilee had a healthy cultural life. The room had been packed. Matthew was there, as were Arvid and his family, the entire Nielsen clan, and the Treases. Even Reverend Wilton and Linnea were there, sitting next to each other.

Plays, concerts, socials, and parties went on regularly, according to Mrs. Jenkins. Rose had seriously underestimated how well established the town was. It wasn't Chicago, but it was far beyond the two-horse village she'd envisioned.

Eric was silhouetted against the side of the building as he leaped into his wagon. Rose paused only a moment before going to him.

"Eric, you showed a real sense of the theater in there. I'm impressed!"

"Thank you. I'm surprised at how enjoyable it actually was."

"I wanted to ask you before you left—I was hoping I could come out to your farm tomorrow. I promise I won't be a bother. You won't even know I'm there. Might I come out?"

He paused so long that she thought for a moment that he wasn't going to say anything, but finally his response was simple. "Yes."

She found herself smiling to the world at large as she walked the entire way back to the hotel, as she got ready for bed, and even as she picked up her Bible for her evening devotions before sleep.

A day with Eric. The idea was teeming with possibilities.

She opened her Bible and found her favorite verse: *"For where your treasure is, there will your heart be also."* When she couldn't sleep, she would lie awake and sort through her life, trying to determine what her treasure was. Over the years it had gone from being her doll to being her new shoes to being—what would it be now? It was intriguing how her interpretation of that verse had changed during the course of her life as her idea of what her treasure was had evolved.

And maybe, just maybe, she thought as she fell asleep, her heart had changed, too.

ع

Eric splashed cold water on his face. He'd need all his wits about him today.

Rose had said he wouldn't even know she was there. What were the chances of that? Whenever she'd been around him, he'd been painfully aware of her presence.

Last night he could have told her no, he wouldn't be home, but he'd long ago made an agreement with God that he wouldn't lie. Not anymore. He'd already told enough lies for a lifetime, and the last one was the worst. A lie never lived on its own. It had fingers that stretched into every part of his existence.

He'd barely wiped his face dry when he heard the distinctive sound of Big Ole's clopping hooves. "And we're off," he whispered to himself as he went out to meet her.

At least this time she didn't have on those worthless little shoes she'd been wearing before. Instead, sensible brown leather boots poked out from under the hem of her green-flowered skirt.

He was going to clean out the stable today before the sun got too high in the sky. Then he was going to go back into the fields and check on the crops. If there was time, he'd weed his garden and fix the wheel on the wagon that was wobbling.

He had the whole day planned out nicely. Without preamble, he told her the schedule, and she nodded. "Sounds good to me. I can help you, too," she chirped happily as she headed for the stable.

Eric contented himself with rolling his eyes. He could picture how effective she'd be with the day's tasks.

"How's Downy?" she asked as soon as she got to the barn door.

"Growing bigger, but that's what ducks do."

"He's not in his cage." She stopped and frowned at him.

"The duck is all right. He's swimming down in the creek now."

"Do you think it's safe for him to be out of his cage?"

He fought back a laugh. "This is the country, and he's a duck. The ducks go in the cage only at night, and that's only to protect them from predators."

Her forehead crinkled with concern. "I'm not sure that it's enough, but I'll have to trust you."

"I appreciate it," he responded dryly.

Amazingly, she was a tremendous help, and she pitched in fearlessly, even when it meant digging in the dirty straw of the stable. Noon came earlier than he expected, and with it, a problem arose. What would they eat?

"I'm sorry," he began, "but I have to say that I don't have much for us to eat. I usually grab what I can and bring it with me."

"That's not a problem," she said, running her hand over her sweat-stained forehead. "I'm not particular."

Not particular? He thought back to the day he'd met her, how she'd been so impeccably dressed and so very elegantly out of place in Jubilee. Now she was sitting in his barn, scented with the odor of the stable rather than expensive perfume, her calico dress smeared with dirt, and she was beautiful.

He shoved the thought out of his mind. Food. That was what he needed to focus on.

Within minutes, they were sitting on the front step of his home, eating bread and cheese.

"That breeze feels good," she commented as a waft of air lifted a stray lock of hair from the side of her face. "I must look terrible."

He swallowed. "No. Not at all. You look—very nice."

She smiled at him, and he felt as if he were fourteen years old again, awkward and ill at ease around women. "Why, thank you."

The curious ducklings waddled toward them, begging for bread.

For a moment, neither of them spoke as Rose threw bread crumbs for the ducks; then she said, "I don't know much about you."

Every muscle in his body stiffened. "There's not much to know."

"Oh, I'm sure there is. Everybody has a story. If they didn't, I'd be out of a job. I'm interested, for example, in where you lived before you got here."

"I already told you that I wouldn't—"

She waved away his words. "I was horribly pushy that day, and I'm sorry. I realized that I was trying to force you to do something. Now I'd rather that you see on your own how important it is."

He had to step very carefully. He had to stay with his promise to God not to lie. "I thought your story was about homesteading."

"It is. But my readers will want to understand what brought you out here. Was it wanderlust? A desire for a better life? Greed?" Rose leaned toward him. "Can you help me understand?"

"People homestead for many reasons," he said. "Those are probably the prevalent ones."

"And which was yours?"

She was persistent. Either he'd have to answer her question, or he'd have to divert her attention.

"What is yours?" he asked her.

She stopped and stared at him. "My what?"

"Your motivation for coming out here. Why did you do it? Why did you choose me? What do you want?"

"I don't see what this has to do with—"

"I'm trying to show you that there isn't a simple answer, not for you, not for me."

He stood up and tore his bread into shreds, which he tossed toward the ducks. He had to end this conversation.

"Let's get back to work."

eight

When you feel this open to God, it is tempting to believe that all is wonderful, all is good, and all can be believed. It is not so. As much as we wish otherwise, it simply is not so.

Rose groaned as she climbed the stairs to her room at the Territorial. She had never worked so hard. Every muscle in her body screamed for relief. There was nothing she wanted more than a hot bath and sleep.

How did people do this every day? She'd be lucky if she were able to move at all the next day. Eric, on the other hand, seemed tired but invigorated at the end of the day.

He was quite an enigma, this man of the prairie. He had adeptly deflected her attempts to discover information about his past. If he thought this would deter her, though, he was mistaken.

She'd wanted him to answer at least a bit about his life so she could have directed the conversation toward his life as a physician—and why he'd abandoned such a noble career.

Of course, she didn't have to know all that for her series to succeed. But if she could find out, it would make him come alive on paper.

A young woman bearing hot water came into her room. As she filled the small tub in the room—a real luxury in the Territorial, Rose had found out—the maid chattered away. "This must be worlds away from Chicago. What are the stores like? How full are they wearing their skirts now? We don't have much here, but that doesn't mean I have to look like an urchin, at least that's what I tell my ma."

Rose's mind was so exhausted that the talkative young lady's words made little sense. She opted for nods and murmurs at what she hoped were appropriate times.

"I guess there are fancy restaurants in the big city. Have you ever eaten at one? What are they like? Do you go to the theater?"

Rose stifled a yawn. "I don't—"

"You have the most glamorous job ever. Writing the society column must be lots of fun! How did you get your job at the newspaper? I don't think anybody else here had quite as exciting a job. Well, there was an actress, Laura something, but she didn't stay. And Mr. Johansen, of course, but it's mainly that cloud of suspicion, you know, that makes him so mysterious."

"Suspicion?" Suddenly she was wide awake.

The young woman tested the water with her elbow. "There. That should do it."

"You were talking about Eric Johansen?" Rose prompted.

"I was?"

"You said something about a cloud of suspicion."

"Oh, that." She wiped up a spot of water that had dropped on the floor. "I don't know anything for sure, just that he didn't leave wherever he was without some question about something or the other. Something that wasn't too good, if you get my drift, but I don't know what. That's all. Have a good sleep, Miss Kelly."

And with that, Rose was alone—and wide awake.

❧

Eric looked across the field warily. There was no sign of Big

Ole anywhere on the horizon. Maybe Rose wasn't coming out again today.

It had been almost two weeks since she'd come out and worked with him. It stunned him to think of it that way, but that's what she had done—worked with him.

He hadn't seen her since then. He hadn't made it to church thanks to a latch on the ducklings' cage that hadn't hooked properly. Sunday morning he'd spent in a torrential downpour trying to corral them from the places they'd chosen to roost.

His worship service had been private and very personal and heavy with thanks to God for keeping the ducklings safe during their nocturnal explorations.

The weekend's rains had kept him indoors, which was in its own way a blessing. One of the things he hadn't expected in farming was how frequently things broke. Reins snapped, bolts got stripped, and wheels cracked.

He'd taken the time of solitude to fix what he could. He'd hammered and patched and nailed until at last he'd accumulated a satisfying pile of repaired items.

He hadn't been able to mend everything, though. His stove was a cranky old thing, and the time had come to replace it with something more reliable. The oven door didn't seal properly, and he tended not to use it during summer since it made the kitchen—and the rest of the house—unbearably warm.

As the days got hotter, he'd find even less reason to cook or bake, but he told himself, as he combed his hair and checked his shirt for spots and stains, that there was no future in delaying the inevitable. He'd need a new stove come winter. He might as well start shopping for it now. No sense in putting it off.

Plus, an annoying little voice told him he might, just might, run into a certain newspaperwoman with hair the color of the sunset and eyes as green as a poplar leaf.

He pushed the notion from his mind. Rose Kelly was nothing to him—and he was nothing to her. He'd seen her type before: the woman who had her goals in sight and would let nothing—and no one—interfere. But more importantly, he'd seen softness in a woman, a woman who. . .

Eric let the thought trail away unfinished. Some areas of the past were totally unproductive to revisit. This was one.

He shoved his hat onto his head, but when he got outside, he took it off again. The recent rains had left the air humid and heavy. By midafternoon, the sun would have baked all the moisture out. It was looking to be a scorcher.

Quite a crowd had gathered outside the general store when he arrived. "What's going on?" he asked one of the children who was standing on tiptoe, trying to peer through the window.

"It's that singing lady," the boy answered, bobbing back and forth in an effort to see inside.

" 'Singing lady'?"

"That woman from New York City. She's singing tonight at the town hall, remember?" The boy craned his neck farther. "Oh, look! There she is. Wait! Here she comes!"

Charlotta Allen glided through the door of the store like a grand ship sailing into port. Feathers plumed from her green sequined hat perched atop hair that was an unnatural shade of blond, and her purple velvet dress was crusted with thick ivory lace. Red boots peeked out from under her hem.

"Wow," the boy breathed in awe, "I can smell her from here."

Eric tried to disguise his laugh with a cough, but he wasn't successful, and at the last moment as his laughter hung in the air, he saw the horrified face of Rose Kelly over the singer's shoulder.

Suddenly his laughter evaporated, and he tried to cover his embarrassment by ducking his head. Some of the townspeople trailed after the singer as she began her promenade to the town hall, while others returned to their business.

Rose stood a moment, clearly torn as to which way to go. Finally she said to him, "For my article," and caught up with the singer.

He entered the store and choked as the smell of the singer's thick perfume assailed him. Freya Trease raised her eyebrows and nodded toward the street. "I'm thinking of boiling some onions to cover that."

The laughter came back, this time unrestrained.

❧

"It's been a pleasure meeting you." Rose nodded at the singer as she began her vocal warm-ups in the small room at the back of the town hall. Walking as rapidly as she could without running, she fled to the door and practically fell outside, taking in great gulps of fresh air.

Eric was standing off to the side, talking to a cluster of people, and he grinned when he saw her. He spoke briefly to the others and came to join Rose.

"Needed a breath of unperfumed air?" he said.

"Desperately. It wouldn't be so bad, except I don't think she's bathed in weeks. There just isn't enough perfume in the world to cover that—although Miss Allen certainly has tried."

He smiled. "It'll be interesting when all of Jubilee crowds in there. It's going to get a bit close, I suspect."

Rose shuddered. Just a few minutes in the store and then in the town hall's back room with Charlotta Allen had been a few minutes too many. She'd had an idea that an interview with the singer would make an interesting sidelight with her articles, but she was more than ready to abandon that angle.

"I can't," she whispered. "I just can't."

"You know," he said, "it's going to be packed in there. They'll probably have to open the doors to keep it fairly cool. We could sit out here and listen."

"What a wonderful idea! There's even a bench there already."

Rose thought back to what the chambermaid had said, about Eric's leaving under "a cloud of suspicion." She hadn't been able to puzzle it out. What could he have done that was so terrible?

And was she safe—working with him at the farm? Sitting with him tonight? They would be within shouting range of the audience if something happened. At his place, she'd have to be especially careful.

After everyone had gone into the building, they sat on the bench. "Do you think they'll miss us?" Rose asked, quite aware of his presence beside her. In contrast to Charlotta Allen, he smelled wonderfully of soap and sun.

"If they do, they'll be jealous that they didn't think of it."

Jealous because they're not sitting next to Eric.

Someone came and propped open the door. "Sorry there aren't any more seats in here, folks. We're plumb full up."

"That's all right," Eric called back. "We'll enjoy it out here."

"Absolutely," Rose added under her breath.

The first notes of the concert spilled out of the hall into the evening air. Rose recognized the piece: It was an aria from *Carmen*. She had heard it performed several times in Chicago, but never quite like this. The notes wobbled and exploded as Miss Allen sang.

"Is it supposed to sound that way?" Eric asked.

"Not exactly," she hedged, trying to be charitable, but the expression on his face stopped her. It was a mixture of disbelief and surprise. "The truth? Not at all."

"Good."

"Good?" She stared at him. "Why would you say that?"

"I was afraid my ears had gone bad."

"They might if you had to listen to this every night." Rose clapped her hand over her mouth. "That was mean. I'm sorry."

"No problem." Eric leaned back and looked at the sky. "No more rain, I guess."

"That would be a nice relief. I spent the weekend in my room at the hotel, working on the articles and even reading a bit." She didn't tell him all she had done—which included a lot of daydreaming about a certain farmer with the brightest blue eyes she'd ever seen.

She needed to change the subject. "Is Downy all right? I worried about him in the rain," she said.

"Rose, he's a duck. He likes being wet."

"I suppose."

The aria crescendoed to a thundering end, and the diva launched right into another operatic selection. At one time, Charlotta Allen might have been a talented soprano, but her voice was past its prime, her range too limited to perform solo works.

The thought that the woman was traveling through small towns in the Dakota Territory, reliant on heavy perfume for hygiene, saddened Rose.

"Do you have a family in Chicago?" Eric asked.

She sat up straight, glad for the interruption of her dreary thoughts. "What an odd question."

"Why is it odd? You've asked me."

"Yes, but I was interviewing you."

"And now I'm interviewing you."

"Fair enough. Yes, I have a family. My parents are still very much a part of my life—and of me. I think I take after my father. He's big and boisterous and opinionated."

"You're not big." Only when he chuckled did she get what he had said.

"Go away." She punched his arm lightly. "Sometimes I wish I were more like my mother, except I couldn't live in the shadow of my father the way she does. Still, she's as quiet and strong as he is loud and strong. I love them both. What about your parents?"

"Are you asking as Rose Kelly, reporter, or Rose Kelly, friend?"

How could she answer that? Was there any way to pour five years of living for the newspaper into one sentence? One paragraph?

"I've been writing for the *Tattler* for five years now," she said. "It's part of who I am. When I'm Rose Kelly, friend, as you put it, I'm also Rose Kelly, reporter. It's difficult, though, with us, since you're not only Eric Johansen, friend. You're also Eric Johansen, subject."

"So can the four of us find happiness together?" he asked lightly.

"Only if you trust me," she answered. "And only if I can trust you."

He reached across the bench and took her hand. "I don't know, Rose. I just don't know."

Rose's emotions tumbled over each other in a chaotic riot. What was happening? Was he saying he couldn't trust her—or she couldn't trust him?

Praying had always settled her soul. That was one thing that Katie Kelly had taught her daughter. Even her father had told her about the importance of prayer, but he put it in more commonplace terms: "When you need help, Rose, my love, go right to the top."

It was good advice.

Dearest God, she prayed, *help me see what I need to see. Help me be what I need to be. Can I trust him? Can I?*

She knew what she wanted the answer to be and why.

Eric Johansen was holding her hand.

nine

We do not all see with the same eyes. Nor do we hear with the same ears. A story told again and again loses its truth as it passes through the mouths of the tellers and the ears of the hearers.

The audience began to stream out of the town hall.

"It's ended," Eric said, torn between happiness that the booming music had stopped and sadness that his time with Rose was almost over.

People walked by them, nodding as they passed. "Well," he said, "maybe it wasn't as bad as we thought. They're smiling."

After Mrs. Jenkins, Linnea, and Reverend Wilton, who were talking in a cluster as they strolled out of the hall, had greeted them cheerfully, he realized why they had all been so jovial. He still had Rose's hand in his.

There was no graceful way out of it. He stood up so suddenly that he nearly knocked the bench over. Rose righted herself—and the bench—and asked, with a upturned grin, "We're leaving?"

"It's late." He cleared his throat. "I'll walk you back to the hotel."

Among the last stragglers coming out of the concert were some of the women from church, who whispered among themselves before approaching the bench. "So nice to see the two of you together. It's a lovely night for romance,"

Mrs. Jenkins said as she walked by them.

Romance? He'd put up with the church women's match-making efforts, borne them in silence, but this was too much. He knew he should say something, but he couldn't respond. Something dreadful was happening in his throat.

He didn't dare look at Rose. What must she think of him?

"Well." Rose broke the silence. "That was a little more than I expected."

"I'm sorry—"

"No need to apologize for someone else's words," she said briskly. "I'm sure you've done nothing to encourage that notion. Besides," she added with an impish turn to her lips, "maybe she was referring to herself. Is there a Mr. Jenkins? I don't believe I've ever met him."

"There is. He's a quiet sort, doesn't go out of the house much. He's a real bookish fellow and spends much of his time with his personal library. Mr. Jenkins isn't a regular churchgoer, but once in a while, you'll see him there."

"See? Maybe she was inspired by the music to spend some time with her husband."

"You give that concert too much credit. It wasn't really music, and it wasn't much inspiration."

They continued to discuss the evening's entertainment as they strolled back through the town, carefully avoiding any mention of Mrs. Jenkins's comment. The air was gentle, with no hint of the earlier humidity.

Their fingers brushed as they crossed the street in front of the hotel, tempting him to take her hand in his. Instead of inches separating them, though, there was a chasm. He'd overstepped earlier. It wouldn't happen again.

His hand felt empty, and he clenched it tightly against the ache.

At the door of the Territorial, she shifted her little bag from one hand to the other, as if hesitating. "Thank you."

The words took him by surprise. "Thank you? For what?"

She touched his arm and looked him straight in the eyes with those glorious green eyes. "Thank you for sitting with me."

"It was my pleasure," he began, letting his heart soften. From the glow in her expression, she'd enjoyed the evening as much as he had. Maybe, just maybe, this could work out.

"And thank you for working with me on the articles. If you don't mind, I'd like to shadow you some more later this week."

He felt as if she had slugged him in the stomach. So much for the love of a lifetime. He was her subject. How could he keep forgetting that?

"I'm working in the fields. It won't be very exciting."

"I'm not looking for exciting."

Good. Then we're a perfect match, he thought.

"My next article is almost ready," she said. "I just need some background information about you, what made you come out to Jubilee in the first place, and more importantly, what keeps you here." She opened the hotel door. "And don't think you can weasel out of it, Eric Johansen. I always get my story."

With that, she entered the Territorial's lobby, leaving Eric alone on the street with his thoughts.

The moon was hidden, but the stars shone brightly across the prairie. He hadn't decided which he enjoyed more—a moonlit ride home or a starlit ride home. Either way, God provided light for his journey.

How true that was, he mused while Sir Gray, as his horse was now called, navigated the night road to his home. God had always been there, even when the dark minutes had turned into darker hours. God was his light, constantly staying at his side, guiding him.

The light hadn't dimmed. Oh, there had been times when it seemed to have gone behind a cloud, but all he'd had to do was pray those clouds away.

Now, more than ever, he needed a clear light.

He was terribly confused about Rose. Lately she had said things that made him wonder what she knew. If she knew anything, anything at all, he was done for.

She suspected something. He could hear it in her voice, in the questions that seemed innocuous but were, in fact, quite direct.

Caution. Every day of his life required caution, but that was the price he had to pay.

He'd almost let his guard slip this evening. He couldn't risk that. No, not at all. Yet he'd come so close to letting himself relax. He had enjoyed the evening, but was she just trying to get his confidence?

No matter how doggedly Rose pursued her questioning, no matter how her eyes sparkled like liquid emeralds, he had to be on his toes. If she caught him off guard, all he'd worked for here, all he'd built, would come undone.

The stakes were too high to take any chances—even on love.

A shooting star twinkled its way across the Dakota sky, a moving diamond on velvet. It was a reminder of a promise he had made as he left Boston. He could deal with Rose if he broke his promise, but there were certain things a man just didn't do, and going back on his word to the Lord was one of those things.

There was only way to deal with it all. He had promised

God that he would never lie again, and the easiest way to do that was to say as little as possible.

He slumped on the wagon seat. Why was it that the easiest way was actually the hardest way?

&

It was almost as if he were courting her, Rose thought dreamily as she entered the Territorial. When his hand—

"Rose! Rose Kelly!" Rose heard and smelled Charlotta Allen at the same time. If anything, both her voice and her aroma were more powerful than they'd been earlier in the evening.

"Miss Allen, how nice to see you again. Your concert was quite. . ." Rose struggled for a word that would be truthful and yet not hurtful. "Impressive," she settled on at last. "It was quite impressive."

"Thank you very much. I do so enjoy coming to these small frontier burgs to share my gift." Charlotta lifted her substantial chin proudly. "They are so appreciative," she cooed, "of having any sort of art in their lives."

Rose could only nod in silent agreement. "Any sort of art" was precisely correct as a way to describe the diva's singing.

"I'm about to sit down and refresh my throat with a cup of tea." Charlotta motioned grandly toward a small reception room off the lobby. "Would you like to join me for a late-night restorative?"

"Tea would be nice." It did sound good. She was slowly beginning to adjust to the singer's abundance of perfume.

With a great *swoosh* of lace-embellished velvet, Charlotta Allen led Rose to the reception room where the same young chambermaid was setting the table for them.

"Ma'am," she said, with a little curtsy that encompassed both the singer and Rose. Rose couldn't help noticing the way the maid's bright, mink-colored eyes took in every detail of the singer's clothing and hair. She was sure that within a day the young woman would have shared it all with her friends and family.

After they were seated and served with an elegant silver tea service and blue willow china—which Rose suspected did not appear for most guests—Charlotta swirled her tiny silver spoon in the delicate cup and asked with an air of nonchalance, "Who was that dashing young man you were with, dear Rose?"

"Dashing? Oh, you must mean Eric. He's a homesteader here."

"He's quite handsome."

"I suppose he is," Rose answered warily.

"Are you two"—Charlotta swirled her forefinger in the air—"romantically involved?"

"No!" The word shot out of her.

The singer leaned over the table and patted Rose's hand. "Please don't take offense. I'm just such a snoop!"

All of this was leading somewhere. Rose could tell that the singer had something on her mind. All she had to do was be quiet and let Charlotta speak, and eventually she'd learn what the diva's motives were.

"He looks somewhat familiar. More tea?" Charlotta held up the silver teapot.

"Yes, please." *I'll stay here and drink tea until I'm a sloshing mess if necessary,* Rose thought. *I have to find out why she's talking to me. I think it has something to do with Eric.*

"This is amazingly good tea considering where we are, don't you agree?" Charlotta asked.

"Yes, it is."

"You said his name was Eric?"

"Do you recognize him?" Rose had to restrain herself from screaming. This was going so slowly.

"I think so. Is his last name Jorgeson?"

"No. Johansen."

"Ah." Charlotta nodded. "Yes, that's it. Eric Johansen. From Boston."

"You do know him!"

The singer shrugged. "No, I don't. But I've heard of him. Or read about him." Her painted eyebrows met in a deep frown. "Oh my. I can't quite place where I learned this. Isn't it frustrating when you can't recall something like that?"

"Indeed."

"Ah, it's the price I must pay for traveling around the world with my entourage, bringing sunshine and joy into the drab lives of so many."

Rose bit her lip. Hard.

"But we were talking about Mr. Johansen, weren't we, dear?"

Rose nodded.

The diva leaned over the table, so close that her perfume and various scents mingled in an overpowering miasma. "Yes, I know about this Eric Johansen." She ended her pronouncement with a sharp bob of her head.

"And?"

"Well, I am not the kind of person who goes about gossiping and telling tales, but you are such a nice young woman, so kind and sweet, and I don't want anything to happen to you."

Rose's heart flipped painfully. The chambermaid had been right. Tears pressed against her eyelids, and she forced them back. "What. . .what do you know?"

"He murdered someone."

ten

Perhaps the hardest thing to do is to trust unequivocally.
It is also the most dangerous.

"Excuse me?" Rose put her cup down so sharply that it rattled in the saucer. She must have heard the singer wrong.

"Oh, silly me, I am such a goose. Look at this. I've made you spill your tea." Charlotta pulled a lace handkerchief from her bosom and mopped ineffectually at the linen tablecloth where a pale brown stain spread.

Rose swallowed. Her throat was terribly dry. "Did you say. . .did you say that Eric. . ." She looked around to make sure they were alone, then whispered the words. "Murdered someone?"

"Yes, dear." Charlotta continued to dab at the spot.

"Are you sure?"

"No, of course I'm not sure. This was awhile ago, you understand, and I only saw his picture in the paper."

"Then you might be recalling someone else." The chambermaid had said that Eric left Boston under a shadow, but murder! It didn't seem possible. "Yes, I'm sure you're thinking of another person. A name that might sound similar, perhaps?"

The singer stopped her swabbing. "No, I don't think so. It's not the kind of thing I'd forget."

"Who. . .who did he murder?"

"A woman."

Rose's heart seized. Eric, a murderer? Charlotta had to be mixed up. There was no way Eric had murdered anyone.

"You must be mistaken."

The singer waved to the maid who hovered by the door. From the way she was bent toward them, Rose knew the young woman was desperately trying to overhear them, so she clamped her mouth shut when the maid came over.

"Might we have something to eat with our tea?" Charlotta wheedled. She looked at Rose. "An evening of music does take so much out of one."

Rose bit back the reply that rose entirely too easily and merely nodded.

The maid brought them a plate of cookies, and Charlotta poked through them with a pudgy forefinger. "Raisins. They have raisins in them. I do not like raisins. Ah, well." She sighed and chose one anyway and fastidiously picked out each raisin.

Rose waited with waning patience as the diva dissected each cookie. She seemed to have forgotten the subject entirely.

Finally she could bear it no longer. Making sure the maid was well out of earshot, she brought up the matter again. "You were telling me about Eric. You just told me he is a murdering madman."

"Murdering madman? No, dearest, not at all."

Rose was ready to pound her head on the table with frustration, but she fought for control. "But—"

"Oh, I don't think he could be called a madman." The singer shook her head so vehemently that her earrings swung wildly like erratic pendulums under her improbably colored hair. "He's not a madman." She paused and stared at the teapot. "But wouldn't anyone have to be mad to commit murder?" she asked her reflection.

Rose took a deep breath. Her mother had always told her that a lie brought into the sunshine soon evaporated, and she knew what Katie Kelly would advise at the moment. *Bring out the lies. They'll go away, and you'll be left with the truth.* "What happened? Who did he kill, and why?"

"Aren't you quite the little reporter with your questions." The diva's smile was tinged with a touch of evil. "Well, dear, it was quite the story in Boston." Finished at last with the cookies, Charlotta patted her lips with the napkin and placed it on the table. "Of course, there isn't much to tell. He killed one of his patients."

"Killed a patient?" The room spun dangerously around Rose's head, and she gripped the sides of her chair tightly.

"I don't recall the details at all." Charlotta licked her fingertip and secured the last wayward crumbs on the tablecloth. "Something about a woman. She was a widow, and I think she even had a child or two."

"Why isn't he under arrest?"

Charlotta shrugged her shoulders. "I think he worked something out with the authorities."

Then, as surprisingly as she'd opened the conversation, the singer ended it. She pushed her chair away from the table and stood up. "We travel early tomorrow, so I must bid you good night." She waved her plump hand dismissively and left in a grand flourish.

"Good night," Rose said to the diva's departing back. "Thank you for the tea."

The little maid reappeared and began to clear the table. "I don't think she heard you," she said to Rose.

"No," Rose said, watching as the end of Charlotta's dress vanished up the stairs. She couldn't help but notice that the hem was quite ragged. "No, I don't suppose she did."

She retreated to her room, leaving the young woman to finish cleaning up the remnants of their tea.

As she prepared for bed, she kept turning over in her mind what Charlotta Allen had said. Murder? Could Eric really be guilty of murder?

It didn't seem possible, although certainly she knew that not all murderers were as grotesque on the outside as they were on the inside. Many of them were dangerously charming and used it to their advantage.

Eric didn't seem to fall into either of those categories. Murderer? No, not at all.

But she couldn't dismiss the story out of hand. Some part of it was true; she just didn't know which part. Rose picked up her Bible and found the passage that the minister had used that Sunday. One verse was particularly appropriate: *"The words of a talebearer are as wounds, and they go down into the innermost parts of the belly."*

People's natural predisposition to share their lives through stories had a terrible tendency to lead them into sharing too much. That was, she knew, just a nice way to say that they gossiped.

Rose had covered enough news stories and interviewed enough people to recognize why the singer had felt compelled to tell her the story, even an incomplete one. She'd seen it often—it was the newspaper form of gossip.

George, the editor of the *Tattler*, had his own explanation. He'd shared it with her one night when she'd come back to the paper's offices upset with a source, an elderly man who knew some background information in bits and pieces about a story she'd been pursuing. After four hours of talking to him, she couldn't tell where truth ended and rumor began.

The editor had leaned back in his wooden chair—even in Rose's memory, it creaked—and slowly placed his feet on his cluttered desk and tucked his hands behind his head. *"It's the way some people connect with others,"* he'd said. *"Usually it's the folks who can't make their own relationships work. You know the kind. They don't have friends. Once in a while they have a cat or a dog or even a canary, but that's about as close as they get."*

He'd continued his sensible explanation. Just knowing someone who knew someone made them part of the story in their minds. People's curiosity came partially from caring and partially from nosiness. Either way, he'd pointed out, it was what kept newspapers going.

She sighed. This wasn't good. It was beginning to look like the very trait that made her a success was going to be the thing that brought her world tumbling down around her shoulders.

Rose rubbed her fingers over the gilt letters on her Bible. She was going to need help. Wagonloads of it.

&

The next morning dawned bright and sunny, and Rose winced as she looked out the window. She hadn't slept at all, and her eyes felt gritty. Throughout the dark hours, she'd gone back and forth in her thoughts, turning her options over and over.

She'd come to an uneasy decision.

Rose picked up her little bag and headed out of the hotel, wincing as the dazzling sun sliced into her reddened eyes. She walked resolutely down the street and turned in at the telegraph office.

Just inside the door, a woman who couldn't have been older than her late teens balanced a child on her hip while listening to a middle-aged woman extol the virtues of her new rug.

"Miss Kelly!" The young mother switched the baby to her other hip. From the relieved expression on her face, Rose suspected the woman was grateful for the break in the conversation.

Rose cooed over the round-faced baby, who gurgled happily in response.

The freckle-faced clerk at the counter was deep in conversation with two older men about the likelihood of a bumper crop. "Excuse me a moment," he said to his companions when he noticed Rose waiting.

The men nodded and stepped aside.

"I'd like to send a telegraph, please," Rose said, laying her tiny purse in front of her. She unlatched it and withdrew a folded sheet of paper. "Send this message to Evelyn Roller at the *Chicago Tattler*."

The clerk opened the sheet of paper and scanned it. "Sorry, Miss Kelly, but I can't quite make this word out. What is this?" His stubby finger pointed to a word.

Rose laughed. "That word is 'researcher.' Evelyn Roller is our researcher at the newspaper. My teachers plagued me endlessly about my dreadful handwriting when I was in school. Can you make out the rest of it?"

The young man squinted at the paper. "Well, to be honest. . ."

Grinning, she took it from him and read it aloud. "To Evelyn Roller, Researcher, *Chicago Tattler*, Chicago, Illinois. Please see what you can find out about Dr. Eric Johansen, formerly of Boston. Charged with murder? When? Who? Thank you, Rose."

A heavy silence fell over the room, and Rose realized

with horror what she had just done. The clerk's face was so bloodless that his freckles stood out like splatters of ink. The men stood frozen in place, their hands stopped midmotion.

The baby broke the silence with a wail, and the two women swept out of the building.

"Oh, I'm sorry." Rose's voice cracked. The words were terribly insufficient. "I'm so sorry. I'm sorry."

As she fled the building, she caught a glimpse of Linnea, her hand pressed over her mouth.

She had done some awful things, but nothing as unspeakable as this. She had ruined Eric's life.

≈

Eric scattered grain and watched the ducks race after it. They'd lost their downy fuzz and were now nearly full grown.

What was he going to do with these crazy creatures? He rocked back on his heels and pondered the situation.

How had he gotten saddled with a group of ducks that were supposed to be his self-propagating food supply and that had, instead, turned into very demanding pets? A black-winged insect made the mistake of investigating the strewn grain, and Downy gulped it down.

Maybe he could sell the ducks. Then they'd be off his hands, and the moral quandary about food and pets would be gone.

He snorted. Moral quandaries didn't go away like that. He knew that from experience. He also knew he couldn't run from them. No matter how much he thought he'd taken care of the past, it was forever with him, and now it was finding the most disturbing road back into his life.

Once he would have thought that the world was made up of that which was clearly good and that which was clearly evil, but lately the line between the two was blurring. He'd crossed it once himself and found himself forever stained.

The sound of hooves ended his reflection, and he stood up, groaning a bit as his muscles tried to uncramp. He was getting old.

Big Ole led the wagon right into his farmyard. Rose wasn't even holding on to the reins, he noticed. "You thinking that this horse doesn't need direction?" he asked as he unhitched Big Ole.

Rose patted the huge horse's side. "As if I could tell him anything. It wouldn't matter where I wanted to go. Big Ole decides, and that's where we head off to. For some reason, he seems to think I should be here."

His breath caught in his throat, but then reason took over. Of course she was here. She was observing him for her stories.

She leaned down and scooped up Downy, who promptly nipped her nose. "What are we doing today?" she asked Eric as she rubbed her nose ruefully. "That fellow has quite a bite."

"He just ate a bug."

"Oh, good. Are you comparing my nose to an insect?" Her hands shook a bit as she put the duck back on the ground.

"Are you all right? Did Downy hurt you?"

She stared at Downy as he waddled away in apparent indignation. "I think I offended him by holding him."

"He's the king of the duck yard," Eric answered. "I think he'll recover."

"Will he?" Her voice sounded different, almost as if she were unsure.

"Rose, he's just a duck."

Rose turned to him. Her mossy green eyes pooled with tears. "Eric," she said, "I've done the most hideous thing ever. I don't know what to do."

Eric did the most natural thing he knew. He wrapped his arms around her and held her against him, let her cry out her pain against his shoulder in great gulping sobs until his work shirt was wet with her tears.

His cheek against her hair, he murmured wordless comforts.

"I'm so sorry," she said, her voice muffled against his chest. "I'm so sorry."

"Shhh, shhh. It's going to be fine."

"No, it isn't."

"Shhh." His head turned a bit, and he found himself lightly kissing her sunset-colored hair.

He knew it then. He loved her. He would do anything for her. He couldn't stand this anguish she was feeling.

"Shhh, Rose. Shhh, my love."

She pulled back and looked him squarely in the face. "Eric, you can't love me."

"But I do." The freedom the words gave him was astonishing. "I love you, Rose. I love you."

She wrenched free of his grasp. "This is what I have done. I said that you were a murderer—well, I didn't say that exactly, but I said enough so that now everyone will think you're guilty, and to make it worse, I said it at the telegraph office, and now—now, oh, I don't know what will happen now, but you have every right to hate me." The tears began again. "You have every right to hate me as much as I hate myself."

His mouth moved, trying to form words, but none came out.

"Say something," she whispered. "Say something. Don't make me leave in silence."

He turned and walked into the house, his heart shattered on the ground.

eleven

In silence we can hear the most clearly. We must, however, prepare ourselves for what we might hear.

The solitude of the prairie suited Rose's mood. More than anything, she needed to be alone. She dropped the reins and let Big Ole ramble as suited him. Eventually the horse would take her back to Jubilee.

Guilt washed over her like a blood-warm wave. She'd done some imprudent things before, but this was more than that.

She put her face in her hands as if she could blot out her actions. Why, why, why hadn't she thought before she read the telegram aloud?

Or more to the point, why hadn't she just asked Eric?

True, he hadn't been at all open to her inquiries about his past, even the mildest of her questions. And what would he have said to her if she *had* asked him? *"Yes, Rose, I killed someone. Would you like some tea?"*

Still, she should have asked him, shared the story she'd been told, given him the chance.

Perhaps she could blame it on Jubilee. In Chicago, it wouldn't have mattered. There if she'd heard a story like this, she simply would have gone back to the *Tattler* offices, done a bit of research, and had her answer. But here, having to rely on the telegraph for research—

She shook her head. She couldn't justify that train of

thought. The problem wasn't the telegraph. It was her rashness.

What had been her strength was now her weakness. She'd turned her impulsive words and her inquisitive nature into her trademark style, a style that had never affected anyone else. But now the consequences were dreadful.

Big Ole slowed at a fork in road, as if asking her which way to take.

"Don't ask me," she said to him. "I seem to have developed a talent for doing exactly the wrong thing."

The horse snorted as if in response and plodded on.

A meadowlark's melody poured across the prairie, a liquid song that held the promise of another summer. Even as the notes caressed Rose's ears, the sound of the grass in the endless Dakota wind was dryer, crisper than it had been when she first arrived.

Autumn was on its way. Her time in Jubilee was more than half over. By Christmas, she'd be back in Chicago, happily making the rounds of holiday parties and not worrying a bit about a man whose life she had destroyed.

A man who'd said he loved her.

The cruel irony struck her. He had held her close, told her he loved her. Those first tender moments of spoken love had been destroyed by her confession.

The wind picked up, and Rose pulled her shawl closer around her shoulders. There was definitely a touch of the season's end in the tendrils that crept in under the edges of the soft wool.

Winter—and then she'd leave. The thought clawed at her. How could she leave Jubilee, leave Eric?

But how could she stay?

Her fingertips toyed with the strap of her tiny purse. She

felt so alone, so small on this vast land.

The words she spoke when she first went into Redeemer Church came back to her. She'd told Eric, "God hasn't forgotten me. Why would I forget Him?"

She wasn't alone. Not at all.

Rose knew what she had to do. There on the road between fields and grass, she bowed her head and prayed. *I'm not even sure what to ask for. You know what I need—and what others need. I've caused so much sorrow and suffering. I wish I hadn't done it, and I don't ever want to do it again. Please help me.*

She lifted her head and opened her eyes. Somewhere on the land that stretched into tomorrow was the man she had hurt. The man she loved.

Even the prairie didn't have enough room to hide that fact from her.

A tear dropped onto her purse, blotting a single petal of the embroidered flower with a dark, wet blemish. Maybe she should go back to Chicago and try to forget all that had happened here. She straightened in the wagon, and Big Ole whinnied questioningly at the sudden movement.

That was it. She would return to Chicago and forget about the man with the Dakota sky in his eyes.

Or she could flap her arms and fly to the moon.

❧

Eric sat in front of his house, watching the sunset. He hadn't gone into Jubilee in almost six weeks, not since Rose had made her grand pronouncement in the telegraph office and ruined his life.

September was a gentle month. The days were shorter, and it was time to start thinking about bringing in the potatoes. The wheat was done, harvested when the August sun had baked it to a golden perfection.

Or maybe he'd be best to leave the crop in the ground and simply take his leave. He'd run before. He could do it again.

He could come up with a story to cover his tracks. Not lying, exactly. He could take bits and pieces of the truth and rearrange them into something that would satisfy the wagging tongues and silence the terrible stories.

There was, of course, that pesky problem with his vow to tell the truth. No, he wouldn't lie, no matter what fancy name he put on it.

He could hear a horse coming toward his house, and he stood up, his heart filled with ridiculous hope. Maybe it was Rose come to tell him it was all a mistake, that she loved him and they could—

It was Reverend Wilton. He alighted from his horse with studied caution. "Evening."

"Evening." Eric went out to greet his visitor. This wasn't the first time the minister had come to visit him, and it probably wouldn't be the last. He knew what was on the man's mind.

The minister strolled over to the duck cage. "These fellows have grown mighty big."

"Sure have."

"I believe they're larger than Arvid's. What are you feeding them?"

"I feed them grain, but they get a good share of insects, too."

"Ah. That might be it." The minister continued to study the ducks.

Had simple conversation ever been so. . .not simple? Each exchange seemed to be pulled from the depths of the speakers.

"That one by the corner there, he's fine looking." He was pointing at Downy. "Are you by any chance thinking of selling him?"

"No." As soon as he said it, Eric recognized the folly of it. Of course he should sell Downy. In his mind, that was Rose's duck, and Rose had effectively ended whatever relationship they might have had.

"Are you sure?"

This was his chance, but he said, "The duck's not for sale." Reverend Wilton would think he'd gone around the bend for sure if he'd explained: *Well, you see, I can't have the woman I love, so I'll keep her duck instead.* And maybe he had.

The minister nodded. "To tell the truth, Johansen, I'm not here about the ducks. We haven't seen you in church for quite a while, and I guess we both know why."

Eric swallowed hard. He met Reverend Wilton's gaze squarely. "Yes, sir, we do."

Neither man spoke for a while. Then the minister asked, "Do you want to say anything?"

Eric shoved his hands deep into his pockets as he tried to corral his thoughts. "No."

After another pause, Reverend Wilton said, "Johansen, that's not good enough. I'm sorry, but it's not." He leaned down and pulled a stalk of grass from the ground and bit off the end of it. "I can't think that's the truth, your taking someone's life, but I can't defend you if you won't defend yourself."

Eric's heart pounded, but he spoke slowly and quietly, hoping to deflect more questions. "I haven't asked you to defend me."

Reverend Wilton chewed on the grass stalk a moment, staring out across the fields. At last he spoke. "Murder is a serious charge. I don't care if you were a teacher or a policeman or a pickpocket before you came out here. None of us do. Just as long as you play fair and treat people square. That's the way we live. For all of us, this is our second chance at life, at getting it right."

Eric didn't trust himself to speak. The words probably wouldn't make it past that lump in his throat.

"We've been friends for a long time. I know that you've been fleeing from something in your past, something that's been pulling on your soul so hard that you can't shake it, and I've never asked what it is. My job isn't prying. My job is letting people know that when the burden is too big, they don't have to bear it alone. You know that, don't you?"

Eric nodded.

Reverend Wilton sighed. "I can't feature you as a murdering man, Johansen," the minister continued. "But the townspeople are asking questions, and I think they deserve some answers."

He was right, and Eric knew it. But the bonds of his sworn silence kept him from sharing his past. He lowered his head.

The reverend put his hand on Eric's shoulder. "The people of Jubilee have respected you since you arrived. You're a hardworking man, a Christian man by all accounts, and we're feeling blindsided by this news. All you have to do is explain it to me—even a brief accounting would do—and I can go back to town and reassure the folks that you're exactly what they've always thought. That would clear your name."

Still, Eric stood mute, trapped in his promise.

"I don't have to tell them the story. All they need to know is that everything is all right. That's all."

"There's nothing to tell," Eric muttered, realizing that

everything he'd built here in Jubilee was tumbling down around his head like a castle of sand.

Reverend Wilton's lips tightened into a straight line. "Again, Johansen, I can't help you if you won't let me." He got back on his horse, and as he picked up the reins, he turned to Eric. "Even God can't help you if you don't ask Him."

Eric stood motionless as the minister rode away. If only he knew how many times Eric had prayed, how many times he'd fallen to his knees. . . .

And it wasn't that God hadn't answered. No, He had. Loud and clear, God had answered.

જ

Rose stood in the small kitchen of the church. Clouds of steam billowed around as four large pots of potatoes boiled on the stove in preparation for another lefse-making session. The harvest potluck was the next morning

Harvest! Had time ever flown so quickly? Already the first flakes of snow had started. Soon she'd be leaving Jubilee. . .and Eric.

It had been more than two months since she'd exploded his life to smithereens. She hadn't seen him at all. She hadn't dared go out to his farm—she couldn't face him, couldn't stand to see him turn from her as he surely would.

He hadn't been to church, but she'd heard through the Jubilee grapevine that he met with the minister privately.

An unseen hand clutched at her heart as the enormity of what she'd done struck her again.

"Stirring works a bit better if you move the spoon around," Mrs. Jenkins said at her shoulder, and Rose came back to reality with a thump.

"Sorry. I was lost in thought." Rose vigorously swirled the large wooden spoon in each of the pots.

Mrs. Jenkins bobbed her head in response and moved on to supervise a small cluster of women who were examining something very closely.

She'd made an uneasy peace with the people of the church. She'd explained over and over what had happened, how she was simply trying to get to the bottom of a nasty rumor, and after a while, she was accepted back into the fold—tentatively.

If she could disappear inside this billow of steam, she would. As it was, the privacy it afforded her was welcome. The townspeople were pleasant enough toward her, but underlying everything they said or did was a sense of distrust. Even Linnea, who was among the group in the corner, had pulled back from their friendship.

"I made these last night," the schoolteacher told the others. "I found the directions in *Ladies' Home Companion*."

"What are these things?" Mrs. Jenkins asked the women. Rose eavesdropped shamelessly. It was better than returning to her thoughts.

"Napkin rings." Linnea had been carrying a box when she'd come into the church, but she hadn't told Rose what was in it. The box must have held the napkin rings.

A bustle at the door told her someone had arrived.

"Since when does a napkin wear jewelry?" The booming voice belonged to the minister, and Rose turned to watch him, obscured by the steam's pluming fog.

The women greeted Reverend Wilton, who picked up one of the napkin rings and held it in front of his face. "What does this thing do?" he asked.

Linnea took it from him. "I'll show you." She rolled a dish towel and inserted it inside the ring. "You stick the napkin inside the ring, like this." She held out her handiwork.

"Can you tell me why? Oh, I understand. We need to imprison the napkins so they don't escape."

Even without seeing his face, Rose heard the laughter in his voice. But there was something else, an undercurrent of happiness that ran between Linnea and Reverend Wilton.

The answer hit her full force. Linnea and the minister were in love!

How had she missed it? Had Linnea said anything? Or had Rose been too self-absorbed to hear?

She flushed as she remembered when they met for the first time and Linnea mentioned someone in her life. Rose had dropped the subject to begin questioning the teacher about Eric.

There was another disturbance at the door, a scuffle of boots across the wooden floor, and then the minister's voice rang out. "Eric Johansen, don't try to sneak past. I understand these ladies are making your favorite food, and I can't believe you'd walk away from fresh lefse."

Rose quelled a sudden urge to duck under the table. She couldn't see Eric, not now, not in front of everyone.

Quickly she surveyed her options and realized there was only one. She was going to have to stand where she was and make it through the meeting no matter how awful it was going to be.

One lock of copper-colored hair had escaped its bun in the heat of the kitchen, and she tucked it back into place as best she could. Then, with a quick wipe of her palms on her capacious apron, she pasted a smile on her face and stepped away from the steaming potatoes.

"Hello, Eric."

twelve

The air is filled with many things. Insects. Snowflakes. Words that never should have been spoken. Despite the openness of the prairie, the air can be just as thick here as it is in the most crowded city.

It wasn't possible for time to stop, to hang suspended in the atmosphere like a thick fog, but that was how it seemed.

Rose's hands clenched into fists, loosened, clenched again. Her cheeks cramped from her artificial smile, and inside, her heart boomeranged around like something gone wild.

Say something, she bid him silently. *Don't turn around and walk away. Please don't do that.*

Eric's gaze was stony. "Hello, Rose."

"How are you doing?" The basics of conversation were the most she could manage.

He didn't answer immediately, as if he were weighing what to say. At last he simply nodded. "Fine."

"And Downy?" She must be out of her mind, worrying about the duck at a time like this.

"He's grown up."

She was suddenly aware that everyone was staring at them, their eyes switching from speaker to speaker as if they were watching a play.

"Well," she said, turning back to the potatoes and stirring them with unnecessary force. "Well."

Behind her, the discussion picked up again.

"I've never known Eric Johansen to pass up lefse fresh off the takke." The voice belonged to Mrs. Jenkins.

"I'm not staying," he answered. "I came in to fix that floorboard again, but I've got to get back to the farm."

"Take some with you. Here, take this package."

Rose turned and saw Mrs. Jenkins press something into Eric's hands. He took it, thanked her, and left as quickly as he'd come.

She handed the spoon to another woman. "The potatoes are almost done. I need a breath of cool air. Do you mind taking over for a while?"

Without waiting for an answer, she rushed from the kitchen into the yard outside the church. The snow had turned to rain, and the wind whipped the heavy droplets against her face. She didn't have a coat on, but the rain-drenched air felt refreshing after the heat of the kitchen.

Eric had unhitched his horse and had one foot in the stirrup.

"Wait!" she called to him. "I want to. . ."

What did she want? She had no idea, just a vague knowledge that he couldn't leave like this with so much unspoken, so much at stake.

He stopped and turned to face her. When she reached his side, he said, "I really don't have anything to say to you."

"Maybe not, but I have things to say to you."

"You've already said enough."

His words struck through her like a lance, and she sagged.

"Eric, I know. I wish I could take it back."

"Well," he said, finishing his mount and grasping the reins, "you can't."

She put her hand on the horse's halter. "Eric, I'm sorry."

"Maybe."

Forgive me, she begged him with her eyes. He studied her face, and for a moment she thought he might soften. But instead he said, so softly that she had to strain to hear him, "I'm done here."

"Done? What do you mean?"

He turned away from her and spoke into the rain. "I'm leaving Jubilee."

She watched him ride away through the rain, his collar turned up against the chill wind, until he was only a speck on the horizon.

How could this have happened? How could she have fallen in love with a murderer?

And now he was leaving her.

Her tears mingled with the raindrops as she stood in front of the church, trying to keep herself together as her world crashed around her.

"Rose?" Linnea spoke behind her. "Rose—"

Rose turned into the outstretched arms of the schoolteacher. "I'm sorry, Linnea. I'm so sorry. I made such a mess of everything. It's cost me everything. Eric is leaving, and I don't—" She closed her eyes against the wave of pain. "I don't even have your friendship."

"That's where you're wrong, Rose," Linnea said. "True friendship can survive the greatest storms, and we've been through a wild one. You're my friend, and you always will be."

In the corner of Rose's heart, a little flame of hope flickered.

❧

Eric threw logs into the fireplace to take the chill out of the room. Winter was coming early this year; he could feel it.

At last the kindling caught and began to burn the bark on the underside of the log. Soon enough the log would catch fire, and the small house would be quite warm.

He poked the logs, making sure they were stacked correctly; then he pulled his chair closer. Through the window he could see Downy leading a parade of the other ducks through the downpour, pausing occasionally to nab a surfacing earthworm.

He was going to have to find a home for the ducks. They were too domesticated to leave them here to fend for themselves. Maybe he'd take Reverend Wilton up on his offer to take Downy and the rest of the ducks, too.

Leaving wasn't going to be easy. He'd put down roots here. He'd built this house, farmed this land, made friends.

He picked up his worn Bible and held it in both hands. The words in it had taken him through times of deep despair. He ran his hand over the plain black cover. It was split along the spine, and he thought idly that he should try to repair it.

His first visitor in his new home had been the minister, and Eric would always remember what he'd said. "A good man has a tattered Bible." Well, his Bible was almost in shreds, but somehow Eric didn't feel overly good.

None of this was fair. He didn't deserve what was happening to him. He was caught in the middle of so many webs, all of them based on one horrible day six years ago. He'd done what he'd had to do, and for the rest of his life, his actions would follow him around like an unshakable weight.

He'd never escape his past. All he could ever hope to do was stay one step ahead of it.

He bowed his head and prayed intently. *Dearest Lord, I don't understand why my life will always be ruled by what happened in Boston. I did what I thought I needed to do—You know that—and today, I still think what I did was necessary. But now, here I am, the unforgivable, unable to forgive someone else.*

A log snapped in the fireplace, and he opened his eyes. That was it, after all. He couldn't forgive Rose, and in fact, he didn't know if he should.

He stood and walked around his house. His heart was here on this farm, yet he had to leave. By the end of the week, he would be gone. He had no idea where he was going, just that the time had come again for him to outrun his past.

꒰ꙫ꒱

"No!" Rose stared at Linnea. "You're wrong. No!"

Linnea clasped her friend's hands. "I heard it from the postmaster earlier this morning. He bought Eric's plow. The Fredericksons bought his furniture. Last I heard, he was working out a deal with Mark—Reverend Wilton—about the ducks."

Rose shook her head vehemently.

Worry creased Linnea's forehead. "Rose, you knew that."

"I didn't think he'd leave Jubilee. Not really. And not this soon. I really thought he'd stay and it would all work out when I left to go back to Chicago." She bit her lip. "Oh, none of that's true. That's what I hoped would happen, but of course that's not going to."

"It's more complicated than that. Murder isn't something you just sweep under the rug."

"He can't go." Rose began an uneasy pacing across her hotel room. "He has to stay here."

"Because you're here? Rose, isn't that a bit unfair?"

"There's nothing about this that's fair." Rose sighed. "My mother used to say, 'Least said, soonest mended,' and I'd roll my eyes at her. What did Katie Kelly know, anyway?

I make my living saying things. I talk and I write. What did I care about mending anything? Now I know. Do I ever!"

She strode to the window and looked out. "Did he say where he was going?"

"No."

The prairie stretched ahead of her, its land now carved by the harvest, ready to sleep through the winter. In a few weeks she'd be back in Chicago, in her comfortable apartment with fancy restaurants, wonderful shows, extraordinary parties, and a skyline cluttered with buildings.

She could put this behind her, forget the man who had taken her heart, and start again. People did it all the time. That's what the folks in Jubilee had done, after all. They'd left their pasts and begun their lives anew.

Until she'd come into their midst.

Rose strode to the wardrobe and pulled out her coat and hat.

"Where are you going?" Linnea asked.

"To see Eric. I have to do something right while I'm here, and I think this is it."

The schoolteacher tugged at Rose's sleeve. "Rose, I'm not sure about this. It's too cold today. Didn't you feel the bite in the wind? It's not like summer when you could go off—"

Rose spun around and faced her friend. "I'll be fine. You worry too much. But this is something I have to do."

૨૦

Eric stood in his house. It looked cold and almost sad without the pictures on the wall and the books on the shelves. He'd left his chair and his Bible by the fireplace. Most of the other furniture had been sold or given away.

As soon as the minister came and got the ducks, he could

toss the chair in the back of the wagon, put his Bible at his side, and leave.

The sound of a horse and wagon in his yard ended his musings. Reverend Wilton must have come for the ducks.

He threw open the door and stopped. It was Rose. She was trying to do something with Big Ole's harness, and he came to her rescue.

"What are you doing here?" he asked as he fixed the leather straps. He knew he sounded ungracious, but he wanted to. Being impolite was, he told himself, a small exchange for her ruining his life.

Rose didn't speak but went on into his house. He followed her.

"Can I ask what you're doing in my house?"

"It's true, then." She stood in the middle of the nearly empty room. "No books." She touched the empty shelves. "No painting of the battle of Jericho. You're leaving."

"Yes, I am."

"It's what you want to do?"

"I'm not sure I have any choice."

"You do. Of course you do."

"What choice would you have me make, Rose Kelly?"

"You can stay."

"And you can go. Is that it? I stay here, and you go. It works out quite well."

Rose frowned at him. "That's not nice."

"Not nice? Not nice?" He was overcome with the urge to laugh. "Who are you to say that I'm not nice?"

"I told you I'm sorry."

He leaned against the wall and studied the fire that was burning low in the hearth. "Well, that ought to do it, then. You ruin my life, say you're sorry, and we're off to have tea with the Queen? Is it that simple?"

"Might I point out that you ruined your own life?" Rose snapped back at him. "I'm not the one who makes the news. I just report it."

He didn't trust himself to speak for a moment.

His heart had turned to stone, and it hung like a heavy weight in his chest. So this was what love did to people.

He'd never been this close to sharing the story with anyone. Maybe she'd understand, but more likely she'd put it in her newspaper. He couldn't trust her, not with his heart, not with his life.

Instead, he straightened up. "Go. Just go."

She glared at him through narrowed eyes. "You had the chance to be loved, Eric. I'm not sure you've ever known what that means."

"I know what love is."

"Do you know what it means to love someone?"

"Yes."

"And do you know what it means to be loved?"

His answer didn't come so readily. "What I've known of love has nothing to recommend it," he answered at last. "It doesn't seem to be a productive emotion."

"I thought I loved you," she said, "but I never should have let myself do that. You can't escape yourself, and until you do, you will never be able to love."

"Go. Leave. Get out of my house." Anger shook his voice. "Good-bye."

thirteen

This is the land of second chances. If we are offered the opportunity to start anew, we must ask ourselves: Will we do it differently? And will we do it better?

Hurt washed over Rose in a hot wave. Tears sprang to her eyes, but she turned away quickly. He was not going to see her cry.

She lifted her chin and walked to the door, her back straight and proud. Silence forged a hardened gap between them that words refused to bridge. The only sound was the whistle of the wind as it blew across the prairie, carrying tiny hard flakes of snow that burned into her cheeks as she prepared the wagon and left the homestead. . .forever.

If he watched her leave, she didn't know it. Pride kept her facing forward, and she got again on the road to Jubilee.

She fought back the tears. This was a love that was destined for failure from the very beginning. She'd been deluding herself to expect that anything could come of it.

Especially, her conscience reminded her, *when you ruined his life.*

The winds increased, and she pulled her scarf farther over her face to protect it from the stinging flakes. The snow became heavier, and she peered from the cave of her scarf, watching the prairie become a swirl of white.

She'd come to Jubilee expecting to make her mark in the newspaper world with these articles, so different from her society-page items. She'd never foreseen that what would happen would be that she'd find the love of her life and then destroy him.

Nor had it ever crossed her mind that she'd lose her heart to man who was a murderer. Or was he?

She still hadn't heard from Evelyn Roller, her research assistant. There was the chance, after all, that Charlotta Allen had gotten the story garbled. She seized on the idea and held it close to her heart.

If that were the situation, it would solve everything. She would announce that she'd been mistaken, she'd gotten wrong information, and it wasn't actually this Eric Johansen who'd killed someone, and within minutes the entire populace of Jubilee would know. In this prairie town, news spread like wildfire through dry grass.

She'd be forgiven, Eric would be forgiven, and she could stay in Jubilee.

Stay in Jubilee. She smiled. It was exactly what she wanted to do. She wanted to stay in Jubilee with Eric—if he would have her.

Maybe an answer had come while she was gone. Suddenly she needed to get back to the telegraph office to see if Evelyn had discovered anything yet.

Big Ole plodded along more slowly as the snow covered the ground. She flapped the reins at him and shouted over the wind, "Let's go!"

The huge horse came to a complete stop, dropping his head against the wind-driven snow. Rose snapped the reins again, and then she saw the problem. Big Ole's harness had come apart.

She got out of the wagon and waded through the rapidly accumulating snow. She took off her gloves and held them in her teeth as she tried to reconnect the metal grommets and the leather straps.

"If I could see what I was doing," she said to Big Ole, who stood patiently, his ears twisted back as he listened to what was going on behind him, "I might be able to do something." But as fast as she could work, the airborne snowflakes landed faster on her eyelashes and her hands and the gear.

She leaned against Big Ole's warm side. "I can't fix it well enough to get us back to Jubilee. We're closer to Eric's house." She led the horse in a U so that they were heading back toward the farm.

For a while she walked with him, guiding him with his bridle until she realized that he'd probably be better off without her assistance.

"Big Ole, I don't know if horses pray, but people do."

She buried her face against his flank. *My life has become one long series of trials, God, and here I am, in trouble again. I shouldn't have gone to Eric's house, and then I shouldn't have left it. Guide us home.* Big Ole neighed softly. *Both of us. If not for me, for Big Ole. He shouldn't have to suffer just because I'm a ninny.*

Rose climbed back into the wagon and dusted the snow off the seat as best she could. "Take me to Eric," she called to the horse. "Take me to the farm."

Big Ole tossed his head and began his slow, ponderous walk, taking them, she hoped, to safety.

❧

Eric paced in front of his fireplace. Rose's words spun around him like bees. She loved him! She'd said she loved him!

He'd been so wrapped up in his own anger that he hadn't let her words penetrate. She loved him!

Stunned by this revelation, he sank into the lone chair

in his living room. If she loved him, and he loved her, then maybe, just maybe, their problems could be resolved.

Oh, who was he kidding? He'd just told her to leave.

He'd stood at the window and watched her ride off. She hadn't looked back at all. Once, a patient had told him to turn his face to the future, not to look over his shoulder all the time at the past.

That patient had been the one who had changed his life in so many ways. She was so intricately enlaced in his life that every moment she was there. At night, her pale face, drawn with illness, haunted his dreams. During the day, she trailed his footsteps, asking if he regretted what he had done.

He pushed the memory away. She'd been right. What was in the past were only shadows. He needed to turn his eyes toward the future.

Rose had said she loved him. Then she would understand. He would tell her the truth, tell her what had happened in Boston.

One of the first Bible verses he'd ever memorized as a child came back to him: *"And ye shall know the truth and the truth shall make you free."* He smiled. That was the way he'd learned it, without punctuation or pause, all done in one breath.

He'd tell her—if he got the chance. Somehow they'd work this out.

It was as if a load had been lifted from his shoulders. What was it he'd heard many times? A weight shared was a weight lifted?

If—and he realized how tentative the word was—she agreed to talk to him again, he could stay here in Jubilee. This was where his heart was, not on the road trying to escape the past.

The resurgence of hope was a wonderful thing, he thought wryly as he looked at his nearly empty house, but it often had terrible timing. Well, he mused, perhaps he could get back his furniture and his plow. Knowing the postmaster and Arvid, they'd be willing to return his belongings.

The ducks were still here, including Downy, who'd taken over the farmyard completely. He smiled. A duck, a silly duck, had taken a place in his heart right next to the woman who had named it, and he'd had a harder time making arrangements to part with the ducks than with the household belongings he'd had for years.

The room was growing colder, and when he reached for the poker to stir the logs in the fireplace, the house shook as a fierce gust of wind caught it in its grasp.

In three steps, he crossed to the window. This storm had come out of nowhere, and it was intense. He couldn't see his own wagon in front of his house. The world was white, all white, no matter where he looked.

This wasn't the first blizzard he'd experienced since moving to the Dakota Territory—but it was Rose's first. With horror, he realized she couldn't possibly have made it to Jubilee before the storm struck.

Stupid, stupid! He should have been paying more attention to the weather. He'd lived here long enough to know the signs—a white sky that hung low, the first flakes of snow, and a rising wind. But he'd been too caught up in his own anger to see what was happening around him.

He tried to figure where she'd be right about now. Midway between his house and Jubilee. At the point of no return.

He reached for his coat but stopped. The storm was so fierce that he'd be lost in it, too, if he went out.

The best thing to do with a blizzard was to stay inside. He'd seen enough cases of frostbite to know all too well what exposure would do. If a man was lucky, he lost feeling in his cheeks. If he weren't so lucky, he'd lose his life.

Like all homesteaders out here, he'd quickly learned to anchor a rope to his house near his front door. The rope, the length of the distance from his house to his barn, would be his lifeline in an extended storm. When he'd first arrived, he'd been plied with stories of men who didn't have the rope, or who had but neglected to tie it around their waists when they went out. Once dropped, he was warned, the rope would whip away in the blizzard's gusty winds, and the homesteader would be left to wander in the icy blasts.

He didn't have to worry about his animals.

His horse and the ducks were in the barn, safely insulated against the storm's fury. The ducks liked to get into the horse's stall, probably because of the warmth, he figured, but lately they'd gotten so fat they couldn't squeeze under the gate. Instead, they'd taken to roosting in the loose hay he'd spread in their enclosure, which he'd moved inside when the nights' temperatures had dropped below freezing.

The only one out in the storm was Rose. He squeezed his eyes shut as he remembered what she was wearing: her usual black coat, a large reddish-pink scarf, and thin kidskin leather gloves. He could only imagine what she was wearing on her feet. There probably wasn't a blanket in the wagon—Clanahan was too stingy to provide something like that—and he was sure she hadn't brought one from the hotel.

Would she know what to do? If she got lost and tried to walk somewhere, she'd be disoriented in this storm almost immediately. In a whiteout, when the snow isolated a person totally and obliterated any points of reference, she could be standing right next to the wagon and not see it.

Please, God, lead her back to me.

ಜಿ

Big Ole's steps slowed until at last the big horse stopped. Rose climbed out of the wagon, bracing herself against the frigid wind. She clung to the harness and made her way toward him.

Her feet sank into a drift, and she realized with horror what had happened. The wagon was stuck in the snow. She knelt and dug furiously with her hands to free the wheel, but to no avail. All she accomplished was getting her vastly expensive kid leather gloves soaked beyond repair.

She stood up and grimaced as the wind caught her scarf and blew it off her face. She seized the end just as it was vanishing from sight. The wind was too strong to tie the scarf back on, so she stuffed it into her coat. Surely somewhere along the way, there would be some shelter where she could put it back on or at least find a break in the blizzard winds.

Her coat collar raised in a nearly futile effort to keep the snow from being driven into her face, she floundered through the drift to Big Ole. "I don't know how I'm going to do this," she said to him, "but I think I'm going to have to ride you back to Eric's farm. I'm going to unhitch the wagon, and we'll have to leave it here."

She unhitched one side of the harness. "Mr. Clanahan can charge me whatever he wants for this, but the fact is, Big Ole, we're not going anywhere except to heaven if we stay here."

She reached across and tried to detach the other side, but her fingers were too cold and stiff.

Awkwardly she clambered across the tongue of the wagon,

talking to Big Ole the entire time. "Just let me unhook you from this side, and we'll be on our way. I have to confess that I've never ridden without a saddle, and I've certainly never ridden any horse as big as you."

The harness had started to slide, and she ducked under Big Ole's belly. "There, I think I've got it now. Just let me get my bag out of the wagon. It's on the seat, just. . ."

The tiny purse was there, but now it was a snow-covered mound. It was close enough to reach if she just stretched. But as she did, her feet lost their traction in the snow, and her body twisted. She felt the sharp pain in her ankle just before her head made contact with the wagon's edge, and then all was black.

&

Eric paced the length of his living room. He could cross it in five steps, and he found himself counting them aloud. "*One*, two, *three*, four, *five*, turn. *One*, two, *three*, four, *five*, turn."

She had to be safe. He wouldn't think of anything else. At the very least, she would have found shelter in another homestead. Thinking of anything else was too dire to even consider.

"*One*, two, *three*, four, *five*, turn."

He couldn't stand it. He was driving himself insane. He had to go look for her. It was foolhardy to go out in this storm. He knew that.

But he was a fool.

He sank to his knees and buried his face in his hands. "God, what should I do? Do I go out there and look for her? How will I find her? Please, dearest Lord, I need some guidance, and Rose—Rose needs Your hand to shelter her from this storm. Please keep her safe." He ran out of words. "Please, God. Please."

With renewed wrath, the blizzard shook the house with a mighty roar. He got to his feet and looked out the window at the snowstorm that was keeping him from her.

The world was entirely white. The sky, the ground, the trees, everything was white. There was no way—

For just a moment, the wind subsided. He blinked and leaned closer to the windowpane to make sure.

Yes, there was something out there, a dark shape that moved, just a bit.

Big Ole!

He yelped with happiness.

The horse had more sense than both of them, and he'd brought Rose back to him.

fourteen

Winter is a deadly season wearing a beautiful dress of white diamonds. It is deceptive and demanding. Do not underestimate its beauty—or its power.

Eric threw on his coat, buttoning it crookedly in his attempt to get it on in a hurry. Hat, gloves, scarf—all went on in a blur.

Rose was back!

He picked up the rope that was already anchored to the porch pole and tied it around his waist. He'd try to get both Rose and Big Ole into the barn and out of the storm. The barn was dry and out of the wind and snow. After she'd recuperated a bit, he'd bring her into the house.

The winds flung icy particles right into his skin, but he didn't feel the bite. Nothing was on his mind except one thing, bringing Rose back safely. If something happened to her, he could never forgive himself.

But God had led him to her.

Thank You, dearest God! Thank You! Now please guide me to her. Let me get her and bring her to me. I can't lose her. I can't.

"Rose! I'm coming! Rose!"

The winds picked up again, but he felt safe, tethered as he was to the house. He'd find her and take care of her. Big Ole was swallowed up by the whiteout, but Eric called, and the horse neighed back.

Good. He was headed in the right direction.

"Rose! I'm coming!"

A tug at his waist told him he had reached the end of the rope. "Rose!" Big Ole snorted, and Eric's spirits sank.

The horse must be a good twenty yards away. It was impossible to judge distance in the storm; every sound was distorted. The rope wasn't long enough.

He didn't dare pray on his knees or even shut his eyes. It was too cold. He shook his hands and tromped his feet, keeping the blood running as he prayed out loud. "What do I do now?" he asked God as he rubbed his hands together. "If I take off the rope, I might be lost, too." He rubbed the snow from his eyes. "But if I don't have her, I'm lost anyway. God, be with me. Stay with me."

The image of Rose, earlier in the summer, sitting outside the barn, going through the harness pieces, sprang into his mind. He'd never really finished that project, and right now the bag was still in the barn, filled with—

"Thank You, God!" he shouted as he made his way to the barn.

He looped and knotted the rope around the latch on the barn door. As he dragged the bag to the door, Sir Gray whinnied from the stall behind him.

"Yes, I'm going to make a rope long enough to take me to Jubilee if I need to," he said to the horse as he spread the contents of the bag on the ground.

He ripped off his gloves, blew on his fingers, and rubbed his hands together. "This goes with this. Buckle this. Tie here." The words ran like a murmur from him as he pieced together the parts.

When at last he had a sufficient length, he untied the rope from the door and knotted it to the leather pieces.

"This should work. It has to work." He anchored the free

end to his waist, pulled his gloves back on, and ventured out again.

Walking in a whiteout was unsettling. Without visual landmarks to direct him, even one misstep could spell his doom. He could be headed for the stream, or for the barn, or even back to his house.

Wham! Or for Big Ole. He'd walked right into the large horse, and he laughed with relief. "I've never been so glad to see a horse before in my life."

The huge horse was standing by the wagon. "Stay here," he told the horse as he felt his way to the wagon. "It's unhitched," he muttered to himself as he realized that Big Ole was standing next to the wagon, not in front of it. "How odd."

"Rose?" he called. "Rose, I'm here. Where are you?"

There was no answer, and he began to sweat despite the cold.

He came to the wagon and climbed in it. He sprawled over the bench on his stomach and felt under it, hoping to come in contact with her black cloth coat, but she wasn't there.

Then he felt something under his leg. It was something small, and almost immediately he knew what it was.

Rose's bag. He pulled it out of the snow and held it to his cheek. It was all he had of her.

"Rose!" he called, but the wind tore the word out of his mouth, and it vanished into the distance.

With sinking hope, he climbed into the back and searched there. Again, Rose wasn't there.

Could she possibly be under the wagon? He peered underneath it but saw nothing.

The winds broke a bit, and he saw that he wasn't far at

all from the barn. Anxiously he scanned the area, hoping to catch a glimpse of a black coat or a reddish-pink scarf or even—he shuddered—a small bump on the ground that hadn't been there before.

There were drifts but nothing else. There was no way to look for her footprints. The wind had already erased his own.

Rose wasn't anywhere in sight. Could she have made it to his barn? The thought buoyed him.

"Come on, boy," he said at last to Big Ole. "Let's check in the barn. Maybe she's there. We'll get you warmed up, too." He grasped the bridle to draw the horse with him, but the horse pulled back in objection.

"What's the matter?" He ran his hands over Big Ole's body. "You don't seem to be injured. Come with me. You can—"

The horse again refused to go.

"Big Ole, move." He pulled with all his might, and the big horse reluctantly moved away. "Get away from the wagon. I don't know why—" The reason Big Ole wouldn't move was right under his feet. Rose was crumpled in the snow beside the wagon, and Big Ole had been standing over her, protecting her from the blizzard.

Eric dropped to her side. Her face was fearfully white, but she was breathing. He scooped her up cautiously and put her across Big Ole's back. "This is precious cargo," he said to the horse. "Let's take her to the barn."

The wind paused, as if catching its breath before another attack, and Eric took advantage of the increased visibility to lead Big Ole and Rose to the haven of the barn. They picked their way through the snow, which was deceptive with its constantly changing patterns. One spot might look flat when actually it was the top of a drift.

Sir Gray greeted them with a gentle whinny. "Yes, it's your old friend, Big Ole. He's a brave horse, so treat him nicely."

With great care, he lifted Rose from Big Ole's broad back and wrapped her in the horse blankets that were draped across the stable's edge. "They don't smell great, but they're warm," he whispered to Rose.

He threw clean hay onto the floor outside the stable and made a bed for her. "I'm sorry," he said as he moved her blanketed form into the hay. "I wish I had better for you, but this is the best I can do right now."

Her gloves were frozen, and he peeled them off and tucked her hands inside the blanket. "That should help. We need to get you some real gloves if you're going to stay in Jubilee."

The words struck his heart like icicles. *If* she stayed in Jubilee. He couldn't think about her not being here.

He began to check her for broken bones, and she moaned in pain when he touched her ankle.

"I've got to do this," he said aloud as he began to remove her boot. Once again she was wearing those absurd little shoes no thicker than a moth's wing. The right shoe wouldn't come off.

"Sorry," he said to her unconscious form, and with a sympathetic wince, he tore the leather apart.

Her ankle was swollen and discolored. His experienced fingers probed tentatively, and at last he covered her foot with the blanket, convinced she had only a bad sprain.

When he saw that she was settled and breathing easily, he swiftly tended to Big Ole, rewarding him with a scoop of oats and draping him with another blanket. "You're quite the hero," he said, rubbing the horse's ears. "Stay here, rest a bit, and I'll take you back tomorrow or whenever we can get through again. But right now, I need to get back to my Rose."

Rose stirred a bit in the bed of hay, and he went to her. Her face and hands were alabaster white and extremely cold. The danger of hypothermia was very real, and as a doctor, he knew that the most effective treatment was to hold her next to him, to share his body heat with hers. Tenderly he picked her up and cradled her in his arms.

He put his lips against her head. Strands of her hair, usually so completely tamed in the strict bun she wore, had escaped their confines, and he smoothed them down.

God, now that I've got her back, let her live.

Taking her away from him now would be unbearably cruel. He clutched her closer and, his words like a litany, asked God one thing: *Let her live. Let her live.*

Outside, the storm abated until only an occasional blast rattled the wooden boards of the barn, while inside a woman slept and a man prayed.

fifteen

Trust is the oddest animal on the prairie. It follows us, dogging our footsteps but always lagging back, just out of reach. Coaxing it to us takes patience and endurance.

At last the storm broke entirely. Early blizzards, Eric knew, often ran out of strength quickly, and this one was no exception. It had been ferocious, though, for seven or eight hours, long enough to remind them of the power of snow and wind.

Eric gently moved Rose back to the hay. She murmured slightly but didn't wake up. His legs were asleep, he discovered as he tried to take a few steps. He frowned. This was happening entirely too often.

"You're getting to be an old man, Johansen," he said aloud.

A drift had built up outside the barn, and Eric had to struggle to get the door open. Finally a mighty shove released it far enough for him to slip out.

He gasped at what he saw. The aftermath of a blizzard never failed to awe him. The last rays of the day's sun glimmered across the dazzling white landscape, and Eric had to shield his eyes against the glare. The snow had lost its threat, and now the ground looked like nothing more than wave after wave of powdered diamonds.

Rose's wagon was just on the other side of the barn. It was stopped at an angle, half-buried in a drift. He shuddered as he thought of how close she had come to dying.

She was going to be fine. The swelling on her ankle had diminished greatly. Her pulse and respiration were nearly normal, and except for a few spots on her face and her fingertips, and possibly her toes, she had escaped frostbite.

There was a bruise on her head, too, where she must have hit it. Her unconsciousness was, he knew from experience, probably due more to the cold than to the head injury. People caught in extreme cold tended to fall asleep, and they often died from it.

A duck quacked loudly, objecting to something inside the barn, and the others joined in. They'd awaken Rose for sure if he didn't make the cacophony stop.

He raced inside and smiled at what he saw. Rose was propped up, with Downy, at her feet, glaring at her with indignation. "I think I rolled over on him."

Eric shooed the duck away and knelt beside her. He ran his hand over her forehead and picked up her hand, wrapping her wrist with his long fingers.

She smiled, a bit lopsidedly, but it was a smile. "Do I have a fever? Is my pulse all right, Doctor?"

"Was I that obvious?" He let the reference to his past as a doctor slide by. That would be taken care of as soon as she was back on her feet.

Rose looked around and frowned. "What am I doing in your barn?"

"You had an accident, but you're all right."

She shook her head and stopped suddenly, putting her hand to her temple. "Ouch. I shouldn't have done that."

"Hurts?" His trained fingers probed in her hair. "No swellings or cuts except for the abrasion and contusion over your eyebrow."

She grinned. "Scrape and bruise, huh?"

Downy watched the proceedings with diminishing interest, until at last he waddled to her feet and bit the tip of her left shoe.

"You rascal!" Rose chided as Downy left them to join his fellow ducks in an exploration of the snow-covered world outside. "He bit my—Eric! Did you see my ankle? It looks terrible! And where's my shoe?"

"You've got a badly sprained ankle. As for where your shoe is. . ." He held it up and showed her the torn leather. "I couldn't get it off you any other way."

Rose smiled. "That's okay. I don't think I could have worn them again anyway, not after getting them this wet."

"Are you ready to stand?" Eric asked, and she nodded. His heart felt so light that it seemed it could fly. "Let me help you. Don't put your weight on your bad ankle. Lean on me."

Rose's hair was straggling free of its usually tidy bun, and her coat was missing a button. The bright scarf was half tucked in her collar and half hanging free. Yet she was the most beautiful sight he'd ever seen.

"I think I can do it." She took a few tentative steps with his help and stopped. "I'm a bit shaky."

He needed no invitation. He swept her up his arms and carried her to the barn door.

"I was just going to ask if I could lean more on you when I walked," she said with a wink, "but this is good. This is very good."

If he had his way, he'd never let her out of his arms.

Or so he thought. By the time he reached the door of his house, he'd waded through drifts that came up nearly to his waist, he'd stumbled over a limb that was partially buried in the snow, and his hat had fallen off. His nose was running dreadfully, and his fingers were numb.

Yet he would not let his dear burden down for the world. He carried her inside and put her in the rocking chair. The fire had gone out earlier in the day, but the room seemed immediately warmer with her there.

He got a blanket and wrapped it around her. She smiled weakly and shut her eyes. "Nice."

"Let me build a new fire."

The kindling caught immediately, and soon the logs crackled heartily. He made tea for both of them. "Do you want some lefse, too?" he asked. "I have some. Mrs. Jenkins also gave me some stew this morning. I'd nearly forgotten. Stew and lefse sure would hit the spot, don't you think?"

She nodded.

As he prepared their supper, he asked her, "Do you remember what happened?"

"To me?"

He chuckled. "Yes, you goose. How did you end up with Big Ole as your tent out there?"

"I don't recall everything," she said. "The wagon—oh, the harness. Something about the harness."

"Clanahan's cheap harnesses come apart way too often," he growled.

"Yes! That's it! I do remember!" She sat forward, her hands cradling the mug of steaming tea. "But then we got stuck in the snow, and I decided to come back here, and I had to unhook the wagon."

He rocked back on his heels. "Rose, that doesn't make sense. Why would you unhitch the wagon? How were you planning to get here? You weren't going to walk, were you?"

"No," she said. "I was going to ride Big Ole."

He didn't mean to laugh, but the image of her tiny person

atop Big Ole's wide back was too much. "You. . .were going to ride Big Ole?" he asked as he fought for control of his laughter.

Her chin lifted proudly. "Yes, I was. What's wrong with that?"

He pressed his lips together tightly and then said, "Nothing. Absolutely nothing. So how far did you get on Big Ole's back?"

"I didn't even get there. I went back to get my bag, and I lost my footing, and—" She paused. "And I think I fell and hit my head."

"And Big Ole came back to stand over you and protect you," he finished softly for her.

Tears pooled in her eyes. "God was certainly watching over me."

He reached across and touched the back of her hand. "He was, indeed."

"How did you find me? You didn't go out in the storm looking for me, did you?" Her forehead wrinkled with concern.

"A bit," he said. "You were just outside the barn—not far away at all."

The creases in her brow deepened.

"The only way I can figure it," Eric said, squeezing her hand, "is that Big Ole was smarter than either you or I, and he started taking you in a circle from the beginning, intending to bring you back here where you'd be safe. And he did. And you are."

She didn't say anything. Instead, she sat in the late afternoon sunlight, her fingers knotting and unknotting as she blinked rapidly.

"I'll attend to the stew," he said quietly. "You just rest."

Rose must have fallen asleep again, for when she woke, the room was bathed in early moonlight.

"Hello, sleepyhead," Eric said. Her eyes adjusted to the diminished light, and she saw that he was sitting in the corner, his legs stretched out in front of him.

"Oh, I'm so sorry. I didn't mean to fall asleep."

"You needed it. How are you feeling?"

"Much better, thank you. My head still aches but not as bad."

"You hungry?"

"Very much."

She watched as he stood and went into the kitchen. When he came out, he had a bowl with a spoon. "Stew from Mrs. Jenkins."

He didn't look like a murderer, she thought as she looked into his clear blue eyes. He couldn't be a killer. He just couldn't be. Not and risk his own life to save her after all she'd done. She wouldn't have blamed him if he'd just left her outside to die.

The stew was wonderful, rich and hearty. "Did you have some?"

"I did."

Neither of them spoke until at last Eric said, "Rose, I owe you an explanation. I hope what I tell you will make you see why I didn't share this with you earlier."

"You don't have to tell me anything," she began, "and—"

He held up one hand. "No. I have to."

"I'll listen."

He stood in front of the fireplace and stared reflectively at the flames. "I was a doctor in Boston. I did pretty well with my practice, and some of the most influential families came to me for medical care."

Rose put the bowl in her lap, the stew untouched, as he continued his story.

"But my favorite patients were those whose lives weren't touched by grandeur or opulence. I treated many who had no way to pay me at all except with their thanks. It was payment enough."

"Eric—"

"One of those patients was a woman, a young mother. Her husband had died in a factory accident before their child was even born, and the woman and her child lived in a grimy apartment in the dirtiest part of town. Yet she kept her rooms and her child and herself cleaner than many of Boston's finest families."

He sighed. "Then one day she got a cold that settled into her lungs. She coughed fiercely, and I begged her to go to the hospital. She wouldn't—she couldn't leave her son alone. He was just a little fellow, barely four."

"There wasn't anyone who could take him, even for a while?" Rose asked.

"It wasn't that. Other family members offered. I offered to watch him myself, but she had a failing. She was proud. No one—not I, not her own mother—could take care of her son the way she could."

"She must have been terrified."

"I think she was. So I did what I could. I left medicine for her. I. . ." His voice broke, and he visibly struggled with the memory before he could speak again. "I left her extra, in case the first doses didn't bring it under control, as often happens. I knew she'd be too proud—and too ashamed that she couldn't pay me—to call me again if she got sick."

He braced his arms on the mantel, his back still to her.

"She was sick, so sick. Her fever was out of control, and I know she must have been delirious. Then. . .her son saw the medicine and decided that if one spoon made her feel better, the whole bottle would make her feel really good, and both bottles would cure her entirely."

"Oh no!" Rose breathed, already seeing where this story was going.

"Yes." His head dropped. "The boy gave her all of it, both bottles. She must have been so feverish that she didn't realize what was happening."

"But why would you. . . ? I mean, how did the story. . . ? That's not murder." Her head was starting to spin, partially from the injury, partially from not eating, but mainly from his revelation.

"No, it isn't."

"So why don't you tell the story? The worst thing you did was have a lapse in judgment, but that's only obvious in hindsight."

He turned around and faced her. The moonlight was bright against the snow, and the illumination that came through the uncurtained window outlined his anguish. "I couldn't let a little boy go through life thinking he'd killed his mother, Rose. He had his whole life ahead of him. I couldn't do it. I couldn't."

She held out her hands to him, and he came to her side and knelt. "I lied on the death certificate. I said she'd died from a lung infection, which was, in a roundabout way, the truth. Her family, though, blamed me, and they were right."

"What do you mean?"

"I never should have left her there, that sick, with just the child to watch over her. I shouldn't have left that much medicine. I was wrong, so wrong. I should have insisted she go to the hospital, insisted her son stay with me, something, anything other than what I did."

"No, no," she said. 'You didn't know. How did the murder charge come about, though? I don't understand."

"I was never charged with murder, but there were enough raised eyebrows and innuendos from her relatives to finish off my medical career. Besides, I just didn't have the heart to stay in Boston and pretend to heal people when I'd just killed someone."

"You didn't kill her."

He shrugged. "That's splitting hairs. No one would expect a child that small to know what to do, and she was so desperately ill. That's why I came here, to Jubilee, to start a new life."

"What happened to her son?"

He looked up at her, a knowingly gentle smile on his face. "Only you, Rose, would think to ask that. I'm glad to say that the little boy has found a good home with a couple who wanted a child very badly. They love him very much, and he's doing quite well."

Tears welled in her eyes as she understood. "You did it, didn't you? You found him a home."

"God did that. I was just His hands."

She picked up his hands and held them to her lips. "They're extraordinary hands, Eric. They can deliver a baby or plant a seed."

"Rose," he said, gazing earnestly into her eyes, "you can't tell anyone. What I've told you must stay between us. I promised God that I would always protect that little boy, and I intend to go to my grave keeping my word."

"I won't," she assured him. "It goes to my grave, too."

"Good. And I also will not lie about it. That was part of

the promise. I pledged to God that I would tell this one falsehood but never again."

She clasped his hands tightly. "You can trust me. I won't tell anyone. I know that what you've told me tonight is an act of faith. I've done everything in the world to make you not trust me, yet here you're entrusting me with the most important secret you hold."

"There's another secret," he said, his eyes glowing with reflected firelight. "I've fought it every inch of the way, but I won't anymore. Rose, I love you. I think I loved you the moment you stepped off the train and into my heart."

"And you caught me, and you've held me ever since," she finished. "I love you, Eric Johansen. With every ounce of my being, I love you."

sixteen

The starlit prairie has no comparison on earth. Each glowing star is a kiss from our Creator.

The moonlit ride back into Jubilee was spectacular. Eric had put Big Ole in his barn for the evening and had hitched Sir Gray to his sleigh.

Such peace had come over him that he could almost imagine the stars singing. Rose looked at him and smiled, and he realized that the sound wasn't coming from the heavens. He was humming.

"Happy?" she asked, her hand stealing out to touch his arm from under the buffalo robe he'd taken from his own wagon.

"I am." There was no way to share with her the enormity of relief he felt, no longer under the burden of his secret.

"Eric, I'm sorry for what I did."

"I know that," he answered, and it was true. He did know it.

"Are you still leaving Jubilee?" Her voice was small and hesitant.

"I don't want to," he answered, not daring to look at her. He didn't want to move away and abandon all he had built, but he doubted he could ever feel that this was really home again.

He'd sooner have his tongue torn out, though, than say that to her. She clearly felt terrible about her impetuous outburst in the telegraph office, and he was not going to say any more about it than necessary.

"Jubilee fits you like a good coat," she said.

He laughed, and the sound rolled across the prairie night. "I can see why you're a writer."

"Well, it does," she protested, "and I promise that I'll figure out a way to set things right with the folks in town."

He shook his head. "I don't know, Rose. Trust me. I've been over this twelve ways to midnight, and I can't see any way to fix it."

"We Kellys are a stubborn bunch," she said. "Just wait. I'll figure out some way to deal with this."

When they entered the lobby of the Territorial Hotel, Matthew gaped at her. "What happened to you? Are you all right?"

"I'm fine," Rose said. "I had a bit of a problem during the blizzard, but thanks to Eric here, I'm safe and sound."

"You need more rest," Eric warned. "I'll talk to Clanahan about getting Big Ole and the wagon back to him."

He wanted to kiss her good night, but he settled for an awkward pat on her shoulder.

❧

He was right, Rose realized. She did need more rest. She was just about to start to get ready for bed when there was a knock on the door.

She opened it and saw the young chambermaid. "Sorry, ma'am," the maid said, "but I'm to tell you there're two men downstairs in the reception room."

"Two men?"

The maid grinned. "It's just the minister and the doctor. I think they're both checking up on you."

Rose quickly fixed her hair as best she could and limped

downstairs to the small room.

The two men stood when she came in.

"We saw Eric, and he told us the story of Big Ole and how he saved you from freezing to death," the doctor said.

"You do know that you're a very lucky young woman," the reverend added. "Blizzards are nothing to be trifled with. God's hand was certainly on you."

"Eric suggested that we come here to visit with you. He's a bit concerned yet about your health, and he wants to make sure you don't have any lingering aftereffects," Dr. Pinkley said. "You look fine to me—a bit worn, perhaps—but we'd all feel more secure if I took a look at the bump on your head, checked your ankle, and made sure you didn't get frostbite."

"I'm not sure exactly why I'm here." The minister peered at her questioningly. "He told us he'd meet us here. Do you know why?"

"Yes." The single word came out in a whisper. "Yes, I think I do. But I can't tell you. I don't know why he said—"

"It's all right, Rose." Eric spoke from the doorway. "I've thought about it, and these two men are not only the safest folks to trust with a secret; they're the only ones who might be able to help us."

He sat next to her, and under the table, she took his hand in hers as he began to tell his story. . . .

❧

The men pushed back their chairs and stood. "I've heard enough," the doctor said. "I'm entirely satisfied that Eric— Dr. Johansen, that is—is not guilty of anything except a heart that is warm and caring."

"I agree," said the minister. "We'll announce that we've investigated and found your reputation to be above reproach.

I believe that for most people, the word of a doctor and a man of the cloth will be sufficient to clear your name, Eric."

"How can I thank you both?" Eric asked, shaking each man's hand.

"Well, the pew where the Nielsen family sits has gotten a bit loose," Reverend Wilton said, "and Grethe Nielsen just told me yesterday that they're expecting the eighth little one come spring. I figure that family alone can keep you busy at Redeemer. Pretty soon they'll be occupying two pews."

"And I sure could use some help when I go out of town. Last year I went to visit my sister in Pittsburgh, and some folks here had the nerve to get sick!" The doctor chuckled. "I'd be honored to have you work with me full time or part time, depending on what you prefer."

"You mean depending on whether I can get my plow back," Eric said with a smile. "I sold it to the postmaster when I was planning to leave."

"Oh, he'll sell it back," Reverend Wilton said with a breezy wave. "I'll talk to him if he gives you any trouble."

"Speaking of trouble," the doctor said with a wink to the minister as the two men stood to leave, "what's this I hear about wedding bells for you and a certain schoolteacher?"

"Linnea? Really?" Rose clapped her hands together gleefully.

Reverend Wilton smiled. "Yes, Linnea and I are getting married."

"Wonderful news, Reverend," Eric said, shaking his hand. "Linnea's a good woman."

The three men discussed the merits of marriage, wheat versus oats, and their hopes for a fairly dry winter, and Rose sat back, smiling. This was home. This was where she needed to be, right here in Jubilee, right here with Eric. She began to relax, and soon she had trouble keeping her eyes open.

She yawned, and Eric apologized. "Here I told you to get some rest and kept you up anyway. Go back to your room and get some sleep. I promise no more interruptions!"

She was so exhausted that the long staircase seemed almost endless, even when she was cradled in Eric's protective arms.

"I prescribe sleep," he whispered at her door as his lips brushed her forehead, carefully avoiding the injured part, and she nodded numbly. All she could think of was sleep.

But what she saw when she went into her room woke her up immediately.

There was a white envelope on the table, with a note on the front: *From the telegraph office.*

She tore it open with shaking fingers.

Nothing. Best, Evelyn Roller.

Rose sank down on the bed and laughed until she cried. Evelyn, dear Evelyn, who was quite slow, incredibly accurate—and very late.

Eric had given her back her little bag, and although the dyes from the embroidered rose had run together and some of the beading had come off, her tiny notepad and pen were intact.

She sat down and began to write.

This is my last article from Jubilee. If there ever was a place that God touched, where He put His fingertip on a plot of land and called it heaven on earth, it is here. The sky and the earth roll on forever, and at the horizon neither sky nor land ends. Instead, they go on farther than the human eye can see, farther than the human mind can comprehend, but not farther than the heart can know.

The people here have welcomed me into their fold. Even when

I made terrible decisions—and I've made some spectacularly awful ones—they were ready to forgive. I can never thank them enough for that.

My mother, the incomparable Katie Kelly, told me time and again when I was growing up that forgiveness is the finest grace, and while I have to admit that at the time I thought those were pretty words but empty ones, now I know that what she taught me is true.

I'm tired as I write this. We've had a fierce blizzard, and I almost died in it. But a homesteader risked his life for me to save my own. You've come to know him through these articles. His name is Eric Johansen.

I arrived in Jubilee with a faith in God that was born into my blood by my parents. Every Sunday, Katie and Patrick Kelly marched me into First Church. I know the apostles' names as well as my own brothers'. I can recite the Ten Commandments, the Beatitudes, and the Twenty-third Psalm.

But nothing prepared me for bringing faith, real faith, into my soul like Jubilee did. Like fine, strong metal, it was forged by fire and grows today.

And certainly I wasn't ready for—

She laid down her pen and rubbed her eyes. She was exhausted, but she had to finish. It was almost done. Just one more paragraph. . .

❧

Big Ole had been returned to Clanahan's, and this time the owner gave Rose a smaller horse hooked to a light sleigh. "Now use some common sense," Mr. Clanahan growled when she got into the sleigh, but his words were gentled with concern.

"I'll keep my eye on the weather," she promised him.

The trip to Eric's farm was easy. The cloudless sky was an

astonishing blue, and the snow still sparkled in a glittering display of jeweled white.

He emerged from the barn when she arrived. "Dim-witted ducks," he said good-naturedly. "They've gotten into the oats and made quite a mess. You'll never guess which one was the ringleader."

She stood first on one leg, then on the other, like an anxious schoolgirl. She knew she was grinning, but she couldn't stop.

"You've got some news?" he asked. "I'm about ready for a break. Let's go inside, and I'll make us some coffee."

As soon as he joined her at the kitchen table, one of the few pieces of furniture he hadn't sold, she laid the sheets of paper in front of her. "I'm going to burst if I don't tell you," she said. "It's either the best article I've ever written or the worst. Here. You read." She pushed it across the table to him.

She watched his face as he read. He didn't smile, didn't react at all, and her heart contracted. She'd gone too far with it. If only she could reach across and snatch back the words!

It was too telling. Too forward. Too honest.

He laid it down. "Are you serious?"

"Yes. No. Yes, yes, I am. Or not."

A grin toyed around his lips. "As long as you're sure."

She sat up straight, trying to regain the last shreds of her tattered dignity. "I'm sure."

He gave her back the papers. "Would you read me the last paragraph, please? I want to hear it from your lips."

She cleared her throat and began to read:

"I have fallen in love with the Dakota Territory, with

the endless blue skies, with the endless wind, with the endless snow. I have also fallen in love with a Dakota homesteader named Eric Johansen. I am here to stay."

seventeen

Love is strong. Stronger than a circus weight lifter. Stronger than a jungle tiger. Stronger than a prairie blizzard. Yet it speaks with a voice softer than a thought—and we hear it.

Linnea fussed with the bouquet of berries and evergreen branches, charmingly tied with a blue and silver streamer that matched the velvet ribbons in Rose's hair. "If you'd waited," she scolded Rose, "you could have had a wildflower bouquet. Getting married in Dakota during the winter limits what I can do."

"This is beautiful," Rose assured her friend. "It looks like Christmas, which it should, since it is. Christmas Eve, that is."

The schoolteacher grinned. "You have such a way with words."

"I'm a bit nervous," Rose confessed. "Does my dress look all right?"

"You look splendid in it. Freya did an amazing job on it, didn't she?" Linnea stood back and studied the ivory lace dress that the shopkeeper had fashioned entirely by hand for Rose. "It looks like a dress you'd find in one of those fancy stores back east, like Macy's."

Rose swirled, letting the material swish around her ankles. "Actually, I saw one like this in Marshall Field's right before I came out here, and Freya managed to figure out what it really looked like from my terrible drawings."

"She's got quite a talent."

"Please tell me that I didn't get any smudges on it. I hadn't planned on it snowing so hard tonight, or I would have brought it over earlier and left it here."

"No, you're perfect. Just perfect."

"I hope so. Everybody's here. Even my brothers." She peeked through the curtain at the back of the room. "Oh no. My father's got Arvid buttonholed about something, or maybe it's the other way around. If my father goes back to Chicago with a duck tucked under his arm, I'll know that Patrick Kelly has finally met his match."

"Rose, honey." Katie Kelly's soft voice spoke to her from the door. "The wedding's going to start soon. Are you ready?"

"Mrs. Kelly, I forgot your corsage!" Linnea pinned an artful concoction of evergreen sprigs and lace onto the soft buttery yellow dress that set off the older woman's gentle gray eyes.

"It's really lovely," Mrs. Kelly said. "Linnea, you are quite a talented young lady. Thank you so much for doing this."

"My pleasure. Let me check on the men and make sure they've all got their boutonnieres on correctly."

When they were alone, Mrs. Kelly took Rose's hands. "Honey, he is the one, isn't he?"

"Yes, Mama, he is."

"Your father and I like him, although you do know that no one on this earth is suitable for you in your father's eyes."

Rose grinned. "Let me guess. He had a talk with Eric."

"Of course he did." The two women shared a knowing smile. "It's a time-honored tradition. He listed all the things Eric is not allowed to do: make you cry, make you sad, make you worry. . . He's got quite an inventory that he went through. He worked on it all the way from Chicago. Whatever the wedding vows don't cover, Papa added it on. He loves you so. We both do."

"I know that, Mama."

"I have something for you."

Katie Kelly leaned down and took a package from under the dressing table that had been set up in a makeshift bride's room. "My mother did this for me, and I want to do it for you."

Inside the tissue wrapping was a pale blue Bible; on the front etched in silver letters were the words *HOLY BIBLE*, and at the bottom, in elegant script, was *Rose Kelly Johansen*.

"It's beautiful, Mama!" Rose breathed.

"Open it, Rose. I've started the heritage page for you."

In Katie Kelly's fine handwriting, the top line had been inscribed: *Rose Kelly m. Eric Johansen, Jubilee, DT, 24 Dec 1879. "Love never fails." 1 Corinthians 13:8.*

"Oh, Mama." Her voice husky as she fought back tears, Rose embraced her mother. "This is perfect. Thank you so much."

Linnea popped her blond head in. "Ready to go, ladies? It's time."

"Any last-minute advice?" Rose asked her mother as she clutched her hands tightly.

"Just this—remember to love him. Keep him close to your heart at all times. And, Rose, honey, if you two pray together, you'll find your path will be easier. But mainly, Rose, love and respect what you two have together."

Rose smiled. "Mama, how could I do anything but that? You and Papa raised me too well."

"Too well?" Katie Kelly hugged her daughter. "I don't know if there's such a thing as that."

"Now!" Linnea whispered. "Here comes Dr. Pinkley to seat you, Mrs. Kelly. As soon as that's done, we're going to have a wedding!"

Somehow Rose got down the aisle, balanced on the strong arm of her father, although she couldn't remember anything except people watching her and the feeling that she was surrounded by smiling faces on every side.

Everyone she had come to know and love in Jubilee was there, all of them wishing her well in her new life.

Eric was waiting for her in front of the altar, looking stylishly elegant in his new black suit. His hair was neatly combed, and he was more handsome than she'd ever seen him. "You're beautiful," he whispered as he took his place beside her.

"Dearly beloved," Reverend Wilton intoned, and with those well-known lines, the ceremony began.

Before she knew it, she'd said, "I do," been kissed by Eric, and was walking down the aisle, her hand in his.

At the end of the aisle, he drew her into his arms. "Well, Mrs. Johansen, how did you like our wedding?"

"I don't know," she confessed. "I was so nervous that the whole thing was a blur. Say," she said, looking up at him teasingly, "you don't suppose we could do it again, do you? I remember saying, 'I do,' but I'm not sure exactly what I agreed to."

"You promised to love me madly for the rest of your life," Eric said. "And make me lefse at least once a week."

"Now that," Rose said, "I can do. Shall we seal it with another kiss?"

"That sounds like a splendid idea." Eric had just bent his head to hers when Patrick Kelly's voice boomed across the church.

"A duck? What would I do with a duck in Chicago? Put it on a leash and walk it in the park?"

❧

News item, Chicago Tattler

Amidst wreaths and candles, Rose Kelly, formerly of Chicago, Illinois, and Eric Johansen, of Jubilee, Dakota Territory, exchanged Christmas Eve wedding vows in Jubilee's Redeemer Church. The former Rose Kelly was an established society page reporter for the Tattler, *recently recognized nationally for a series of articles about homesteading in Dakota. Dr. Johansen is a farmer as well as a physician in Jubilee. We wish the couple great happiness together.*

A Letter To Our Readers

Dear Reader:

In order that we might better contribute to your reading enjoyment, we would appreciate your taking a few minutes to respond to the following questions. We welcome your comments and read each form and letter we receive. When completed, please return to the following:

Fiction Editor
Heartsong Presents
PO Box 719
Uhrichsville, Ohio 44683

1. Did you enjoy reading *Rose Kelly* by Janet Spaeth?
   ☐ Very much! I would like to see more books by this author!
   ☐ Moderately. I would have enjoyed it more if

   _____

   _____

   _____

2. Are you a member of **Heartsong Presents**? ☐ Yes ☐ No
   If no, where did you purchase this book? _____

   _____

3. How would you rate, on a scale from 1 (poor) to 5 (superior), the cover design? _____

4. On a scale from 1 (poor) to 10 (superior), please rate the following elements.

   ____ Heroine   ____ Plot
   ____ Hero   ____ Inspirational theme
   ____ Setting   ____ Secondary characters

5. These characters were special because? _____
_____
_____

6. How has this book inspired your life? _____
_____
_____

7. What settings would you like to see covered in future
   Heartsong Presents books? _____
_____
_____

8. What are some inspirational themes you would like to see
   treated in future books? _____
_____
_____

9. Would you be interested in reading other **Heartsong
   Presents** titles? ❑ Yes ❑ No

10. Please check your age range:
    ❑ Under 18   ❑ 18-24
    ❑ 25-34   ❑ 35-45
    ❑ 46-55   ❑ Over 55

Name _____
Occupation _____
Address _____
City, State, Zip _____

Presents

Great Inspirational Romance at a Great Price!

Heartsong Presents books are inspirational romances in contemporary and historical settings, designed to give you an enjoyable, spirit-lifting reading experience. You can choose wonderfully written titles from some of today's best authors like Peggy Darty, Sally Laity, DiAnn Mills, Colleen L. Reece, Debra White Smith, and many others.

When ordering quantities less than twelve, above titles are $2.97 each.
Not all titles may be available at time of order.